Silent Death
in a Mexican Street...

A *bandido* appeared from nowhere, directly in front of Jessica and Ki, who were pouring kerosene onto a pile of wood beside the town hall.

There wasn't time for Ki to react and his hands were busy, but Jessica moved. Seeing the *bandido* draw his holstered gun she threw her knife at him with deadly accuracy. Ki had spent hours showing her how to use a knife and now that training paid off.

The knife struck the heart muscle, and the bandit staggered back, already dead...

Also in the LONE STAR series from Jove

LONGARM AND THE LONE STAR LEGEND
LONE STAR ON THE TREACHERY TRAIL
LONE STAR AND THE RENEGADE COMANCHES
LONE STAR ON OUTLAW MOUNTAIN
LONGARM AND THE LONE STAR VENGEANCE
LONE STAR AND THE GOLD RAIDERS
LONE STAR AND THE DENVER MADAM
LONE STAR AND THE RAILROAD WAR
LONE STAR AND THE MEXICAN STANDOFF
LONE STAR AND THE BADLANDS WAR
LONE STAR AND THE SAN ANTONIO RAID
LONE STAR AND THE GHOST PIRATES
LONE STAR ON THE OWLHOOT TRAIL
LONGARM AND THE LONE STAR BOUNTY
LONE STAR ON THE DEVIL'S TRAIL
LONE STAR AND THE APACHE REVENGE
LONE STAR AND THE TEXAS GAMBLER
LONE STAR AND THE HANGROPE HERITAGE
LONE STAR AND THE MONTANA TROUBLES
LONE STAR AND THE MOUNTAIN MAN
LONE STAR AND THE STOCKYARD SHOWDOWN
LONE STAR AND THE RIVERBOAT GAMBLERS
LONE STAR AND THE MESCALERO OUTLAWS
LONE STAR AND THE AMARILLO RIFLES
LONE STAR AND THE SCHOOL FOR OUTLAWS
LONE STAR ON THE TREASURE RIVER
LONE STAR AND THE MOON TRAIL FEUD
LONE STAR AND THE GOLDEN MESA
LONGARM AND THE LONE STAR RESCUE
LONE STAR AND THE RIO GRANDE BANDITS
LONE STAR AND THE BUFFALO HUNTERS
LONE STAR AND THE BIGGEST GUN IN THE WEST
LONE STAR AND THE APACHE WARRIOR
LONE STAR AND THE GOLD MINE WAR
LONE STAR AND THE CALIFORNIA OIL WAR
LONE STAR AND THE ALASKAN GUNS
LONE STAR AND THE WHITE RIVER CURSE
LONGARM AND THE LONE STAR DELIVERANCE
LONE STAR AND THE TOMBSTONE GAMBLE
LONE STAR AND THE TIMBERLAND TERROR
LONE STAR IN THE CHEROKEE STRIP
LONE STAR AND THE OREGON RAIL SABOTAGE

WESLEY ELLIS

LONE STAR AND THE MISSION WAR

A JOVE BOOK

LONE STAR AND THE MISSION WAR

A Jove Book/published by arrangement with
the author

PRINTING HISTORY
Jove edition/June 1986

ISBN: 0-515-08581-2

Jove Books are published by The Berkley Publishing Group,
200 Madison Avenue, New York, N.Y. 10016.

PRINTED IN THE UNITED STATES OF AMERICA

Chapter 1

The Cañon del Dios, a time eroded, weather scoured twisting channel of red stone, gaped before the three riders who picked their way across the cactus studded foothills.

"This is it, señor, señorita," the Indian said. "This is the Cañon del Dios."

The Indian's name was Squirrel. He was a Papago, a short, very dark man with his black hair hacked off unevenly. He had a cast in one eye and a crooked foot that caused him to hobble along clumsily when afoot. Just now he was mounted on a stubby, spotted pony, and on horseback Squirrel was at home. He knew this land intimately and he deftly guided Jessica Starbuck and Ki toward the mouth of the great canyon.

"How far now, Squirrel?" the woman with the loose honey-blond hair, startling green eyes, and exquisite figure asked their guide.

"Five miles up the canyon, along the creek, you will see," the Indian answered without glancing back.

Ki was half white, half Japanese. He was a man who had trained his body and his mind so that he was never truly ill at ease. He knew his capabilities and they were remarkable. *Te*, the art of empty hand fighting, was his way of life, a way which subdued the mind and lent an amazing, controlled vigor to his lean body. Such a man does not worry much.

Still Ki was beginning to grow doubtful. They had entered the canyon now. Massive red walls closed them in on either side. A narrow, silent blue creek ran past them, winding through the willow brush and occasional sycamore tree. Crows called to each other from the branches of a twisted tree and took off in a flurry of black wings as the riders approached.

Ki glanced at the blond woman beside him and then lifted his eyes to the canyon walls. Now he began to see the cave dwellings, their windows and empty doorways like dark, watching eyes.

"Jessica," Ki said, and when she looked at him, he pointed to the cliff dwellings above them.

"Is anyone still living there?" she asked their guide.

Squirrel turned in the saddle and shook his head. "Not here anymore. Farther up. Here is where the raiders came. Here is where the slavers took away my people."

Jessica nodded. The cave dwellings, ancient and bleak, hung over them. There were signs of recent habitation nearer the river, on the flats: drying racks for fish, a stand of gradually dying corn, stretched hides on the ground. The slavers had come, however, and these things would be used no longer. The work would be left undone.

That was what had brought Jessica Starbuck and Ki to Arizona this time: the slavers.

There was nothing new in slaving along the Mexican border. It had been going on for hundreds of years. The Apaches were old hands at it, gathering up people from the smaller tribes, driving them southward into Chihuahua and Sonora.

This was different. The cartel was behind it.

The cartel, a power hungry, violent international organization, cast its shadow across youthful America, recognizing the lack of organized law enforcement in the West and rich opportunities.

The cartel had murdered Jessica Starbuck's father and her mother. Alex Starbuck had been a powerful and wealthy man, and he had been too upright to stomach the cartel. In the end they had eliminated him, leaving his daughter, Jessica and Ki to carry on the fight.

Now the fight had come to the Gila River, to the small tribes here.

According to Jessica's informant this slaving operation was far larger, far better organized than any previous one along the border. Hundreds, perhaps thousands, of Indians were being taken south to be sold into bondage. Someone was getting rich from human suffering.

The name Jessica had been given was Kurt Brecht, and that name was quite familiar. Jessica's father had left her a black book with all he knew of the cartel's operations in it. Included was a list of officers, men responsible for the cartel's crimes. Kurt Brecht's name was near the very top of that list.

How her informant had come by that name Jessica would never know now. The informant had been found dead in an alley, both of his knees broken and a dagger stuck in his open mouth.

"We are being watched," Ki said in a low, casual voice.

Jessica's head turned slowly toward him, showing no surprise. "Where?"

"From the bluff to our right. I saw him twice. One man."

"An Indian?"

"I think so. It's only natural that they would have sentries out."

Squirrel, who was a good distance off, heard them despite their low tones. "They watch for slavers," he said.

Ki glanced at the man with some surprise. The Indian

had volunteered to lead them to his people, people he said who knew the slavers and knew where they had gone but felt powerless to pursue their enemies and recapture their friends and relatives.

The slavers, they said, were Mexican *bandidos* working for a powerful man who lived in a great hacienda to the south. Squirrel had promised to find someone to show these two strangers the way.

He had also expressed doubts about Jessie and Ki's ability to do anything about the situation. "One man. One woman. What can you do against an army?"

"Just find someone who knows where the leader of the slavers lives," Jessica Starbuck had said.

Squirrel had peered at the beautiful blond woman, at the tall man who appeared to be Chinese like Sing, the laundryman, yet did not look Chinese. His one good eye had gleamed dully and then the Indian had shrugged.

"I will show you."

The shadows were beginning to gather in the canyon, seeping onto the river bottom to stain the land a deep red-violet. Doves began their homeward flight before a fiery sky. Frogs began to grump in the willows.

"How far?" Ki asked again.

"Soon," Squirrel replied.

The canyon began to narrow. The floor of it started to rise toward the red bluffs where now and then a stunted cedar was visible, hanging precariously from the ancient stone, clinging grimly to life.

The trail they now followed wound through willow brush and sage. A rabbit, startled by the hooves of the oncoming horses, zigzagged away, white tail bobbing.

The bandits were around the next turn.

There were a dozen of them, all armed. As Jessie and Ki entered the small clearing, they emerged from the brush, rifles at the ready. Ki's instinct was to fight, but he could see they had no chance. They had been suckered but good.

Their leader was a vast bearded man with the smells of sweat, leather, and tobacco clinging to him. He had a huge belly, a nasty crooked smile, and black, empty eyes. He wore crossed bandoleers and two Remington revolvers.

Just now he was very pleased with himself.

"Welcome, friends," he said with a mock bow. "Carlos, relieve the lady of her guns. Not the man. He carries no firearms, is this not so, Ki? All the same, Carlos, search the Chinaman. I am told he carries unique and deadly weapons."

Carlos was a nervous, narrow man with long yellow teeth and a huge sombrero. He didn't look sane. He moved to Jessica and slipped the Winchester repeater she carried from its boot. Then he reached for her holstered handgun, the custom .38 Colt. It had a slate-gray finish and polished peachwood grips.

Carlos wasn't looking at the gun much. His hands slid up Jessie's thigh as he reached for her holster. His dark eyes gleamed as he raked her curved, compelling body with his hungry gaze. He stroked her thigh, his fingers creeping higher.

Jessica slipped her boot from the right stirrup and slammed her knee upward into the bandit's face. Teeth cracked and blood spewed from his mouth as his head snapped back.

Carlos staggered backward and then stood rubbing his jaw. A dirty little smile creased his jaundiced face and he drew a long knife from the sheath behind his back. He had started forward when a voice halted him in his tracks.

"Carlos, don't be a fool."

Ki who had been tensed, ready for the fight if it had to come and ready to die to protect Jessica Starbuck, looked to his right to see a tall, sleek Mexican dressed in black come forward three steps. He was in his early thirties, handsome, and well-built. His clothing was clean unlike the rest of the bandits', and his stride was smooth and purposeful.

"You saw what she did, Diego," Carlos said.

"Put the knife away," the tall bandit said. His words were spoken softly, but there was a tone of command in them as well. "Put it away, Carlos."

Carlos glanced at the huge bearded man who shrugged. Slowly the knife was sheathed.

"Now," Diego said, "relieve the woman of her weapons as a gentleman would."

Carlos, eyes dark, moved again to Jessica Starbuck and slid her pistol from its holster. He backed away with the Colt in hand and then moved to Ki.

"He has no gun, no knife," Carlos said.

"Search him," the vast bandit with the beard commanded.

"But, Mono—"

"Search him, you fool!"

Carlos did so, his hands cautiously moving over Ki's body. "I can find nothing, Mono."

"Have him get down," Mono said impatiently.

Ki sat his horse a moment longer, staring at the bandit leader and at the other one, Diego, who stood leaning casually against the shoulder of a black horse. Then he swung down lithely and stood submitting to Carlos' search.

"Look in the vest," Mono said. "That's where he's supposed to carry them."

Carlos gingerly looked into the leather vest Ki wore, finding the hidden pockets there. He frowned, turned, and opened his palm to show Mono what he had found.

"These?" the bandit asked in wonder.

"Those. Get them all."

"But..." They were nothing but star-shaped pieces of steel, razor sharp to be sure, but how could these be weapons? How were they used?

"The Chinaman kills with those. Don't you, Chinaman?

"I am not Chinese," Ki said.

"Oh, yes." Mono laughed. "I forget. Japanese, is it not?"

Ki shrugged. "You know so much about me, I am sure that you know that."

"Yes, I know. It is just that there is no difference, is there?"

Again Ki shrugged. Carlos had taken his *shuriken* to the bearded leader who examined them briefly, nodded, and tucked them in his saddlebags.

"May I ask how you know who we are?" Jessica Starbuck inquired.

"You cannot guess?" Mono asked in surprise.

"Yes, I can. Kurt Brecht told you."

"Did he?" Mono appeared surprised. "And who is that?"

Jessica didn't answer. She looked around her at the circle of grinning bandits, at the tall lean man who was smoking a thin cigar, watching her with frank enjoyment.

"It was a good plan, was it not?" Squirrel asked. The Indian was pleased with himself, with the trap he had triggered. "I brought them to you as I said I would."

"Yes," Mono said without enthusiasm.

"I, Squirrel, brought them to you. I fooled them. And now you will reward me, will you not?"

"Yes," Mono said, "now," and he carelessly drew his revolver and shot Squirrel in the face. The bullet emptied the Indian's right eye socket and the back of his skull exploded. Squirrel was hurled back and lay twisted and bloody in the brush.

"Stupid *indio,*" Mono said. He looked at Ki and then at Jessica Starbuck. Whatever he saw in their eyes apparently satisfied him, so he holstered his Colt.

"What are you going to do with us?" Jessica asked.

Her voice was tight, her green eyes angry.

"Do?" Mono laughed. "Fulfill your wishes, Señorita Starbuck. You came here hoping to find the man who pays us, did you not?"

"You're taking us to Brecht?" Ki asked.

"Brecht? Again that unfamiliar name. I am taking you to the man who pays us for our labors."

"I could pay you more not to take us," Jessica said. "My father was a wealthy man. I'm a wealthy woman."

Mono seemed to think that over, stroking his thick beard. "I do not think there is enough gold to pay me to go against this man. I would only end up like the stupid *indio*." He inclined his head toward Squirrel. "And if you and this Japanese man do not cooperate with us, it may very well be that we shall simply kill you and take your heads with us as proof you have been eliminated."

"*He* wants them alive," Diego said quietly.

"He said only that he would prefer to have them alive, Diego Cardero," Mono said. His eyes flashed in a way that let Jessica know there was contention between the bearded Mono—whose name meant ape in Spanish—and the lean, handsome bandit in black.

"As you say, Mono. But I would not harm the woman if I were you." Diego Cardero's eyes were capable of reflecting menace, too. They did that now and Mono, his lip curled back, watched him. Ki noticed the brief duel of wills, the watchful expressions of the other *bandidos*. Something violent, threatening, passed between the two bandit leaders and then dissipated like smoke.

Mono shrugged. "We will discuss it later. My advice to you, Jessica Starbuck and Ki, is to come without struggle, to do exactly as you are told to do. Otherwise—" He shrugged meaningfully.

"We will do exactly as you wish," Ki said, though he had no intention of doing that, had no intention at all of letting the cartel get its hands on Jessica Starbuck. Mono was watching him dubiously.

The huge bandit leader nodded at length. "*Bueno*. Just so you understand."

"I understand," Ki said, hoping the man did not understand that he would kill before he would allow anything to happen to Jessica Starbuck.

But there was nothing Ki could do just then as he was placed back on his horse and, along with Jessica Starbuck, led out of the dusk shadowed canyon. There was nothing anyone could do—not Ki or Jessie, not the lone figure who still followed them along the rim of the canyon bluff.

Chapter 2

Night settled quickly and in a vast silver spray the stars seemed to shower out of the darkness. The bandits made their camp on a low, eroded mesa three miles south of the Cañon del Dios. Jessie and Ki were fed beef and beans and then tied up again before the circulation had even had a chance to return to their numb feet and hands.

Jessica Starbuck was thrown a blanket into which she managed to roll clumsily. She lay there then listening to the muffled Spanish voices, watching the figures around the campfire pass bottles of tequila from hand to hand.

Ki was sleeping or pretending to sleep. They kept the two of them separated, just as they had during the short ride from the canyon. Jessie tried working her hands, attempting to loosen the bonds, but she had no luck at all.

If she had gotten free, where would she go? What would she do? They were a hundred miles from help and the bandits would simply ride them down again. Still, it wasn't in Jessica's nature to give up. She had been through too much, fought too long, to give in.

She watched and waited. The voices from around the campfire droned on for a long while as the stars shifted. One man rose, yawned and stretched, and went to his blankets, and then another did likewise. They staggered as they walked, and when they rolled into bed, they snored almost immediately. The tequila was doing its work.

Mono was asleep now as was Carlos. Soon the fire had burned to embers and the night went darker still. No one moved in the outlaw camp and Jessica slowly stretched her arms toward her boot. They hadn't found the slender knife she had taken to carrying there. Now her grasping fingers found the handle of the little knife and slowly she withdrew it.

Her breath came in quick, shallow gasps as she sawed through the bonds around her ankles, feeling the rawhide ties fall free, feeling the rush of blood to her feet.

She looked at Ki, who seemed to be sleeping. How in hell was she going to cross the camp to reach him?

Jessica's knife cut through the ties on her wrists and she lay there, trying to still her breathing. She rubbed her hands, bringing back sensation.

If she could get into the brush behind her and circle to Ki's position, silently cut him free . . . It was dangerous, very dangerous, but what other chance did they have?

The horses were up a narrow draw behind the camp. If she and Ki could reach them, there was a possibility they could escape.

Slowly now she rolled over and worked her way across the hard earth, feeling the bristle of dry grass and small stones beneath her hands and knees. A bandit stirred; she froze, her hand clenching the knife. He simply shifted position, grunted, and resumed his snoring.

Jessica went on, reaching the sumac and sagebrush beyond the camp. Her heart was hammering as she moved silently through the brush, gently turning aside branches as she worked her way toward Ki.

A tall man stepped out of the high brush and grabbed her wrist. The silver blade of the knife flashed toward

Diego Cardero's face and Jessica saw that—how infuriating!—the Mexican was smiling. He caught her arm as the knife descended, twisted her wrist, and removed the knife from her angry, clutching fingers.

"Damn you!" she said. Cardero had turned her, drawing her near. Now he pressed his lean body against her and kissed her. Jessica tried to fight free, but Cardero had her blond hair in his hand and he held her head still, kissing her again. Finally he let her go.

"You shouldn't wander around in the night alone," Diego Cardero said. "It is very dangerous, Miss Starbuck."

He was smiling still.

"Bastard," she said sharply and Cardero smiled again, his face starlit and darkly handsome in the night.

"We can be friends," Diego told her.

"With someone like you? With someone who wants to make a slave out of me—or deliver me to Brecht, which would be worse? Why are you doing this anyway? Money, I presume."

"Money." Diego Cardero nodded thoughtfully. "Yes, money. There is a bounty on your head and Ki's. A huge bounty."

"Blood money. Not a legal bounty. Do we look like criminals?" she asked.

"No. But what you are is of no concern to me."

"Only the money concerns you," Jessica Starbuck said bitterly.

"Only the money."

He was still close and holding her wrist. He was a dark and evil thing, Jessie decided. He was also something else, something that she couldn't banish from her mind—something that was in his kiss, the kiss that still lingered on her lips, causing them to tingle; something that had sent little fingers of excitement creeping down her spine.

"What are you doing?" Jessie asked. He had turned

with her, taking her with him along a narrow path toward a low knoll where a twisted, broken oak grew.

"Come with me," was all Diego said.

They walked to the top of the knoll, and when Jessica refused to sit, Diego plopped her down. Jessie sat glowering, angry and frustrated.

Diego stood over her with the small knife in his hand. His feet were spread widely, one hand was on his hip. He held the knife out toward Jessie.

"This," he said, "was a bad idea, very bad."

Before Jessie could move, Diego brought the knife forward and down. The point of the knife imbedded itself in the oak tree and with a twist of the wrist Diego snapped the blade off. He tossed the handle away casually.

"Don't you know what Mono would do if you tried to escape, Miss Starbuck?" Diego took a thin cigar from a narrow silver case and struck a match with his thumbnail. He cupped the match flame and lit the cigar.

"What would he do?"

"You were not listening? He would cut your heads off—yours and Ki's—and deliver them to Kurt Brecht in a sack. Believe me, Mono would do this."

"And what's the difference?" Jessie said. "Brecht will only kill us once he has us."

"I don't know that for sure, but the possibility of death is better than its certainty."

"Death is certain," Jessie replied.

Diego shrugged. "I prefer to believe I am immortal. However, I must take you back to the camp and tie you again."

"What if we're seen?"

"What will Mono do? Nothing. I'll tell him that I brought you out here . . . for a little amusement."

Jessie just glared at the tall, smiling man. She hated him, wanted to kill him, she thought. On another level Diego was appealing: tall, lean, handsome, and charming. He was also a slaver and an outlaw.

"What is it you and Mono do when you're not bullying women?" she asked sarcastically.

Diego shrugged, examining the end of his cigar and blowing gently on the red ember. "Many things," he replied at last.

"Slaving?"

"That is something new. It's over now. Mono doesn't like to work hard, and slaving is work. Mostly we live peaceful lives."

"Gentlemen bandits."

"Not exactly." Diego's smile was thin and a little pained. "We drink; we eat; we do as we please. Money is never a worry. We take from small villages in Mexico. When their food is gone, their tequila finished, their women exhausted, we move on."

"It's a pretty picture."

"Not pretty. It is the way it is. Sometimes Mono will hear of a gold shipment, of a bank waiting to be robbed, of a rich hacienda where no one stands guard with rifles. Then we will ride out. This time," he added, "we heard of you and Ki, of the bounty Don Alejandro has placed on your head."

"Don Alejandro? Who's he?"

"That is what this man calls himself." Diego dropped his cigar and stepped on it. "I have never seen a Spanish nobleman who looked like this man, nor have I ever met one who speaks such paltry Spanish."

"He's a foreigner, then."

"Assuredly. Perhaps he is the Kurt Brecht you mention, I don't know. Last month he ventured across the border on some mission or other. Perhaps he was seen by someone who knew his true name."

"He was," Jessie said.

"Yes? By whom?"

"By a man who's dead now," Jessica Starbuck said coldly.

"A friend of yours?"

"No, a man who used to work for my father, a man who discovered Brecht's name and paid with his life for it. Fortunately, he was able to write to me before being killed."

"Fortunately?" Diego said, pondering the word. "No," he replied, "not fortunately at all, Miss Starbuck. It was most unfortunate for you that this man wrote to you because I fear that by that act he signed your death warrant—yours and that of Ki."

Jessica said nothing. Finally Diego bent over her, gripped her by both arms, and lifted her to her feet. "Hands behind your back, please."

"Diego, I wasn't kidding when I said I could pay as much, more even, than Brecht."

"I did not think you were kidding. Hands behind your back, please."

"If you could get Ki out of camp—"

"Will you give me your hands?"

Jessie placed her hands behind her back and felt strong, sure fingers tie a secure knot. Then, just for a moment, she felt Diego lean against her, chest meeting her back, his hard thighs against her buttocks and that same, cold, inexplicable thrill ran up her spine.

"Come now, silently," he said, pulling away. "It is best if I do not have to tell Mono my little story, best if he does not know you were gone at all."

The entire camp still slept. Jessie was put to bed, her ankles retied, and silently Diego crept away, moving like a lean, dark cat. Jessie lay there, staring at nothing until she felt other eyes on her. She glanced across the camp, seeing Ki watching, silently questioning.

He was awake, had probably been awake all along. Yet Ki had made no attempt to escape, none at all. Perhaps he knew they had no chance.

Dawn was red and blurred by low clouds. The *bandidos* stumbled across the camp, heads full of tequila haze, reaching for the huge coffeepot that rested in the flames.

Mono, squatting with a tin cup in his huge hand, was looking at Jessie when she blinked her green eyes open.

"Get up," was all he said, and Jessica looked down to see that she had been cut free. Ki was standing near the fire, his hands tied behind his back still.

If Ki had wanted to, he could have slipped those ties. Ki's body was a competent machine, a machine over which he had great command.

But Ki hadn't the will to make a move just now. There was nothing to be gained, nowhere to go. In the back of his mind, Jessie knew, must be the image of Jessica Starbuck's severed head traveling south to the hacienda of Brecht.

Mono wasn't the sort of man to make idle threats, nor did he have a wisp of conscience to prevent him from doing just what he threatened.

"There's coffee," Mono said to Jessie. Then he rose, turned his massive back on her, and stumped away.

Diego was at the fire when she arrived, but the tall man looked past her, ignoring her. Carlos, his lips scabbed and swollen, hissed and turned away. He hadn't forgotten, nor would he. His pride was injured. A woman had gotten the better of him in front of other men.

Jessie poured herself a cup of coffee and stood watching the rising sun break through the clouds, feeling the eyes of the bandits running covetously over her legs, deliciously curved bottom, back, and breasts. She could almost feel their lust.

Ki was motionless. A deep frustration was building within him and he refused to let the emotion conquer him, so he quieted his mind, his angry thoughts. He breathed evenly, rhythmically, slowing the racing flow of his blood.

There must be a way out of this, he thought, some way, but not simple blind attack, not wild flight across the red desert.

Ki let his eyes lift to the distances, to the rising sun, to the empty desert flats beyond. He could see the Gila River, flowing narrow, shallow, green toward the south. The south was where Kurt Brecht presumably waited for his henchmen to deliver the cartel's troublesome enemies, Ki and Jessica Starbuck.

Brecht could afford to be generous with his reward offers to Mono and his bandit gang. Whatever he paid Mono would be greatly rewarded by the cartel that had suffered many costly losses due to Jessie and Ki.

Ki glanced at Jessica and then looked nearer, to the eroded highlands where only nopal cactus and stunted cedar, yucca and agave grew. He looked to where he had seen the lone man who was trailing them, who had been with them since Squirrel had led them into the Cañon del Dios.

He was gone again now, leaving not so much as a puff of dust to mark his location. But he was still there. It was no coincidence that he was following the *bandidos*. Who was he? What did he want?

"Let's go, Chinee," Carlos said truculently. He gave Ki a hard shove. "We're riding. Get on your horse."

Ki braced himself and then just nodded. There was no point in teaching this vicious half-wit a lesson. It would only lead to trouble for Jessica Starbuck, and that Ki would avoid at all costs.

"Did you hear me?" Carlos demanded, and by the tone of his voice, Ki knew it was coming. Carlos wanted to hurt someone. His pride had been battered and he was determined to make someone pay for it.

"I heard you. I am going," Ki said.

He turned toward his horse and Carlos struck. He kicked out savagely, driving his boot behind Ki's knee. The pain was excruciating. Ki's knee buckled and he fell to the ground, skidding on his face. His leg filled with fire.

He came automatically to his feet, assuming an aggressive stance, but there was nothing he could do. There were too many of them, and Carlos, his eyes narrowing at Ki's poised body, at the hands held loosely yet menacingly before him, lifted a rifle and cocked it, aiming at Ki's chest.

"What is this?" Mono demanded. The bandit leader stormed to where Carlos stood peering down the sights of his Winchester repeater at Ki's heart.

"He tried to attack me," Carlos said.

"Well, shoot him then. I won't have that." Mono might have been giving the order to swat a fly.

"It wasn't like that," another voice said.

Mono turned to find Diego Cardero, smiling and with a cigar between his teeth, standing there.

"What did you say?" the bearded bandit leader demanded.

"Carlos is a liar. He kicked the man because he needed to kick something. A dog would have served his purpose. Carlos is a small man. He is still angry because the American woman kicked him in the face."

Mono looked from one man to the other, from the assured, handsome face of Diego Cardero to the bruised face of Carlos who still stood, finger on the trigger.

"Ah, do what you want," the bandit leader said in disgust. "My head hurts." Then Mono walked away heavily, leaving Diego and Carlos.

"Leave him alone," Diego said.

"Tell me why, Cardero."

"We need the man."

"His head."

"We need the man. I am telling you that, me, Diego Cardero."

Diego seemed not to have moved, not to have quit smiling. But now Carlos could see that Diego's hand was resting on the butt of his holstered revolver and that the dark eyes of the man had grown cold and threatening.

Carlos hesitated. "What do I care about the Chinaman," he said at last. But he did care. It was the second time in two days that he had been shown up: once on account of the woman, once on account of the Chinaman. Carlos wasn't the kind to forget that.

They would both die. And so perhaps would Diego Cardero.

Ki watched the Mexican walk away, watched the swagger and stiffness of him. That was not the end of trouble with Carlos, he knew.

Diego was still watching Ki. "Better get on your horse," he said.

Ki nodded. Just for a moment their eyes met and Ki sensed something. He knew already that this one was not like the others. There was a soul behind those eyes—perhaps a dark, killing soul, but some sort of spirit lived within the bandit.

Maybe that would help. Maybe.

Ki swung aboard his horse and had his hands lashed to the pommel. Jessie was kept well away from him so that there was no chance of communication.

Mono clambered aboard his roan heavily and sat there with a pained expression on his face. He looked around scowling and then said, "Let's go. There is gold waiting and we have a long ride ahead of us."

They rode slowly from the clearing then, the day growing hot as the sun rose to torture the desert and its inhabitants. Buzzards sailed high against a white sky and Ki glanced at them hoping they were not a foreboding.

They rode silently, slowly, through the long dusty arroyos and across the red desert flats, riding deeper into Mexico, farther toward the cartel lieutenant, Kurt Brecht, who wanted their heads.

And behind them the lone man followed like a phantom, invisible to all but Ki who could only speculate and wonder.

Chapter 3

They rode deeper into Mexico, the sun always present, glaring and white. To their right a low line of chalky mountains lifted from the empty salt flats they now crossed. The horses' hooves crunched the dry ground. Nothing moved on the desert; nothing made a sound but the drifting wind that pushed light sand before it and whispered eerily past the bandits and their hostages.

Ki shifted in his saddle. His arms ached. His hands were still strapped to the saddlehorn of the bay horse he rode and it was impossible to get comfortable. Sweat trickled down his spine and it dripped into his eyes, stinging them.

The bandits were even more uncomfortable. Ki smiled as he watched them. They bent over their horses' necks, grumbling and cursing. The tequila still rode with them and it was making things miserable for Mono and his men.

Ki turned a little to watch Jessica. She held herself erect in the saddle, the wind drifting her hair. She might have been out for a Sunday ride but for the grim set of her mouth.

"Damn this desert, damn this heat," one of the Mexicans said.

Mono said, "Shut up, Arturo."

"Why don't we follow the river?" the bandit asked.

"Because I say not."

Arturo looked away, clamping his jaw shut. Mono was in no mood to explain his decisions. A second bandit, very dark with long black hair, said, "Yaquis, Arturo. They've been drifting north. They'll follow the river."

"What do we care about a handful of dirty Indians?" Arturo asked.

"You don't know the Yaquis, do you?" The look in this one's eyes indicated that he *did* know them. The man looked to be Indian himself, though what tribe Ki couldn't have guessed.

"The horses won't last long without water," Arturo said.

"We'll find water," Mono growled. "Tinaja Caliente, eh, Halcón?"

The Indian nodded. "There will be water at Tinaja Caliente."

The bandits fell silent. Ki watched them for a time longer and then again let his eyes lift to the distances. The desert seemed to go on forever. Now and then they passed red-tipped, thorny ocotillo waving in the light breeze; now and then a jack rabbit, set to running by the approaching horses, loped off across the flats. Otherwise, the world seemed dead and empty.

Ki didn't know this country well. He had never heard of Tinaja Caliente. *Tinajas*, he knew, were natural catch basins in stone where water from the infrequent rains was held. *Caliente* meant hot in Spanish. Was there anything that wouldn't be hot in this country?

They had begun to angle westward toward the chalky hills. These seemed to be the *bandidos*' goal. Ki could only ride on with them, biding his time. Yet how long could he wait before he made some attempt at escape? Something had to happen—and soon. Someone had to make a mistake, offer Ki and Jessica a chance to get away. But nothing presented itself. The bandits were alert and watchful.

They rode toward the hills that loomed ahead across the desert flats.

By sundown they were all exhausted. The perspiration no longer stained Ki's shirt, no longer dripped from his body. The devil wind whipped it away before it had barely formed. Ki's body, deprived of water, seemed unable to muster the ability to replace it. The bay he rode walked with his head hanging. The bandits were in a foul mood.

They found the mouth of a narrow, white canyon and started to climb. Ki's horse balked and Carlos slashed it across the rump to keep it moving up the rocky slope.

"Jesus Christ," Arturo said, "I'm going to die."

"Shut up," Mono snapped.

"Soon you'll be up to your eyes in water," Diego Cardero said, "cool water."

"Christ," was all Arturo could pant in response. The horses achieved a narrow bench and followed a second narrower trail to the crest of a low, barren ridge. The wind raced across the ridge, but instead of cooling them, it simply added to their torment.

"Which way, Halcón?" Mono asked the Indian.

"The gap, ahead," the bandit answered. His throat was dry, his voice muffled. His finger pointed out a notch in the jagged white rocks that stood like ancient sentinels. "Just beyond the gap."

A horse slipped and nearly went to its knees. The ground was uneven and rock strewn. The sun was fading fast, painting the white mountains with subtle shades of purple and orange.

They rode slowly through the gap. Ki's horse lifted its ears suddenly and it blew through its nostrils. Another horse, Diego's, nickered wildly.

"They smell it. They smell the water," Halcón said.

"I wish I could," Carlos muttered.

"I don't want to smell it; I want to drink it, bathe in

it, swim in it," Arturo said. His spirits had risen again.

They emerged from the gap into a narrow valley. There was no grass there at all, only bare white stone and thickets of nopal cactus. A single, long dead oak tree tilted out from its roots near the base of the white canyon walls, casting a crooked shadow.

"Just ahead. Water," Halcón said. Now Ki, too, could see it shining dully in the sunset light.

Arturo's horse broke into a run and he let it run. He laughed and waved his sombrero in the air. He reached the *tinaja* first and swung down before his horse had come to a full stop.

They saw him against the sunset backdrop. He dived for the water. Then he recoiled, grabbed at his horse's reins, and yanked it back. The horse reared up on its hind legs, shaking its head in angry frustration.

"What is it?" Diego asked.

Arturo just pointed.

A corpse floated in the water. Or rather half a corpse. The body had been incredibly savaged, arms and torso flayed, the eyes put out. It might have once been a middle-aged Mexican; now it was a ghastly, rotting, faceless thing.

"Hold those horses away, damn it," Mono shouted. "The water's been poisoned."

"Yaquis?" Carlos asked.

"Who else?"

"But why?"

"For the hell of it." Mono lifted his eyes. "Where's the other pond?"

"Up here." Halcón had clambered over the white boulders to a second elevation. He scrambled back now.

"Well, what's there?" Mono wanted to know.

"The other half of him." He tilted his head toward the body they'd already seen.

"Madre de Dios," Mono said, his voice quivering with rage. "Dying of thirst and those bastard Yaquis do

this. If I ever find them, I'll cut their throats, every one of them. I swear it."

"What do we do now?" Arturo asked.

"Do? Go thirsty. Keep the horses at a distance. They'll be hard to handle tonight."

Jessica Starbuck had been helped from her horse. Ki had been cut free of his saddle. Now they stood together as the little valley went dark.

"Tonight, Ki," Jessie said in a soft voice. She didn't look at Ki but at the sunset.

"It's impossible, Jessie."

"We have to try, don't we?"

Ki looked at the scowling dark faces of the bandits. "Yes," he decided, "we have to try." Even if it meant losing their heads, perhaps joining the dead man in the *tinaja*.

They were immediately separated. The bandits started a small fire. There was only tinned beef and beans again with the few swallows of water which remained in the bandits' canteens to wash the food down. Jessie didn't eat. Ki accepted only a tablespoon of water.

The bandits continued to complain, to curse, and to drink—they were out of water, but the tequila still held out.

"Don Alejandro will pay well for these two," Arturo said truculently, "after this."

"He pays well," Mono said.

"How do we know? Maybe he takes our heads too, eh?"

The bandit leader replied darkly, "No one takes the head of Mono. Don Alejandro will pay."

"If we get there." This was Carlos. The crooked little man was growing more unhappy as things went along. His lips were still puffed, his ego still bruised.

"We'll get there. Shut up."

"The Yaquis—"

"The Yaquis are long gone; if not, they wouldn't have

poisoned water they could use," Halcón said logically.

Carlos glowered at the Indian. He took another drink of tequila. No matter how much of that he drank, he was still thirsty and he knew that tomorrow his body would be crying for water.

Carlos was unhappy. He had been unhappy most of his life—ever since his father had taken to beating him. His father beat him for killing a calf so that he could watch the blood flow, watch the wild eyes of the animal as it died. His father beat him for tearing the clothes off of young Alicia Gomez. Carlos had gotten even. He had beaten his father to death as the old man slept.

He had wandered for a time and then joined Mono, seeking comradeship and perhaps approval, but none of these men were his friends. In fact—Carlos took another swallow of tequila—he didn't like any of them, especially the Indian.

He sat glaring at Halcón as the Indian talked to Mono. Mono listened to Halcón. You would think Halcón wasn't a stinking, half-breed Apache.

Diego Cardero was listening as well. He was perched on a low rock watching Mono and the Indian.

"No place else?" Mono asked.

The Indian shook his head. "No place near enough. Unless we want to go north again, try the well at Fuego. There's no guarantee there's water there, though."

"That doesn't leave us much choice," Mono said. "All right. We'll go to San Ignacio."

Diego's eyes flickered. "I thought we weren't going to stop at any pueblos on this trip."

"We have to have water," Mono said impatiently. "San Ignacio has water. The mission well is deep. The old padres made sure of that."

"I don't like riding into a town with prisoners," Diego said.

"The decision's made. San Ignacio," Mono said. He didn't like having his decision questioned and he was tired. He was too big a man to sit comfortably in a saddle all day.

"There's always trouble," Diego said.

"Trouble! Fun, I call it," Carlos said. No one so much as looked at him.

"Yes, fun," Halcón said almost under his breath. He spat on the ground.

"What the hell do you know about it, you damned stinking Apache?" Carlos asked, lurching to his feet.

"Nothing," Halcón said quietly. His eyes were steady and expressionless.

Mono seemed to enjoy this. "Tell him about it, Carlos," the bandit leader urged. "Tell him about Sonoita."

Carlos staggered forward a little, bottle still in hand. "Sonoita—neither of you two was there—we tore that town apart with our bare hands. We took what we wanted. Women, money, liquor. Three days we had the town." Carlos held up three witnessing fingers. "Maybe we do the same to San Ignacio, eh, Mono? What do you think of that, Diego Cardero?"

"I think it's foolishness. We've got prisoners to deliver. Let's get the gold for them and then do whatever we want."

"I think maybe you are the foolish one, Diego." Carlos returned to the fallen log where he had been seated. He waved a hand. "You and this *cabrón,* Halcón—"

The knife sang across the space between the Indian and Carlos. It stuck in the log between Carlos' spread legs, an inch from his groin, and quivered briefly. Carlos hadn't even seen where the knife came from, hadn't seen Halcón throw it. He looked at the knife and the bravery leaked out of him. Mono laughed out loud.

The Indian walked across the clearing and recovered his knife, showing the cutting edge to Carlos. "Men do not speak to me like that, Carlos," Halcón said.

"All right." Carlos swallowed hard. "I meant nothing. I apologize."

The Indian stood over him for a minute longer and then nodded, deliberately turning his back on Carlos to walk away. Jessica Starbuck was watching Carlos, and for a minute she thought Carlos was going to draw his revolver and shoot the Mexican in the back. But Carlos didn't have the nerve to try it.

Mono, too, had been watching the interplay with casual interest. He had been enjoying it greatly. It took little to amuse Mono. And once they reached the town of San Ignacio what other kinds of amusement would the bandit leader indulge in?

The bandit called Delgado, silent, toothy, and armed with no less than three pistols, came to where Jessie slept, tossed a blanket on her, and walked away again. The others were turning in as the fire burned low and then was extinguished by Halcón. He might have been convinced that there were no Yaquis around, but he was apparently taking no chances.

The night went dark and still and Jessica Starbuck began to work at the ties on her wrists. As time went by, the bandits were getting sloppier at tying her. The last time she had tensed her wrists and held her hands a bare fraction of an inch apart as she was bound. Now she could feel a little slack, very little, but enough to give her some hope.

With the exception of Carlos, who had been sent grumbling to stand an unhappy watch, everyone seemed to be asleep by the time the silver moon rose and Jessica Starbuck had eased her cramped hands from their rawhide ties.

They seemed to be asleep, but Ki could not have been. He was facing her, sleeping on his side fifty feet away. He didn't twitch or open an eye as Jessie made her second escape attempt, moving slowly into the shadows, working her way toward the horses. If they could take the entire string of horses and move silently down the canyon . . . Then what? Head toward the river and water? They would have to take their chances with the Yaquis.

She found the horses and another bit of good luck. Someone, too lazy to unsaddle, had left his horse standing unhappily in the darkness. By the moonlight Jessie saw that a Winchester repeater had been left in the saddle scabbard.

She moved to the horse, looking right and left. She slipped the rifle free and turned at the sound of a soft footstep.

"Ki?"

"No," Diego Cardero answered, "not Ki. I don't think he will be coming now."

"Damn you!" Jessie hissed. She tried to bring the rifle around, but Diego had the barrel in his hands already. He twisted and yanked it up, and the weapon was torn free of her hands.

"Dear one," the man said, leaning toward her, "we have to stop meeting like this."

"Am I supposed to laugh?"

"No, you are supposed to quit trying to escape." Diego's hand reached out and Jessie tried to draw away, but her back met the horse's shoulder. Diego's hand touched her hair, smoothed it back, and Jessica, despite herself, felt a stirring in her abdomen, a tingling begin in her breasts.

"What are you, a devil?" she whispered.

"Perhaps." He was smiling now. Taking her arm, he leaned forward and kissed her, and there was nothing Jessie could do to stop her body from responding, her mouth from returning the kiss with parted lips, her body from meeting his and feeling his solid thighs, hard muscled chest, his growing male need.

"Devil," she said again. "Ki..."

"Simply tied more securely. How does he slip his hands from those ties? Those I did myself; I know they were good knots."

"I must..."

Whatever Jessie felt she must do, Diego's kiss smothered it. When he finally pulled away, she was breathless, her pulse racing. Who was this man? She could feel no evil about him, nothing savage or angry.

"Let's talk," Diego said.

"Where?" She didn't even argue with this tall, handsome enigma.

"The upper *tinaja*."

"That corpse up there—"

"I had it removed. He was buried. Rather a cairn was built. There's no chance of digging in this ground. Come, come with me, Jessica Starbuck."

And he took her hand and she went meekly as if there were no choice. The moon cast long shadows before them and bathed the white rocks with quicksilver. They climbed to the upper *tinaja* and there it was still, beautiful. The pond gleamed with silver light.

"Sit down," Diego said and Jessica obeyed as if she had been mesmerized. Diego sat beside her, and for a time they just watched the silver hills, the distant moonlit desert flats.

"Who are you? What do you want?"

"I want you," he said, and he kissed her again, his hand pressing against her spine, running down to her beltline, drawing her nearer. Jessie turned her head away.

"You said you wanted to talk."

"As little as possible," Diego said. His left hand was on Jessie's thigh now, bringing an incredible warmth.

"Who are you?" she asked again in wonder, her eyes searching his face, his black, laughing eyes. "You're not some sort of lawman, a government agent?"

Cardero laughed. "Diego Cardero! No, nothing like that. I am a wanted man, Jessica, an outlaw."

"Then—"

"Then we need discuss it no more." He gently laid her back and she stared up at him as he leaned near and kissed her throat, her parted lips. His hands cupped her breasts firmly; his eyes shone with desire.

"Jessica, nothing will happen to you, to you or Ki. I promise you that."

"How can you?"

"Believe me. I mean it."

Before she could ask another question, he had pressed himself against her. Slowly he opened the buttons of her white silk blouse, his lips following his fingers down, kissing the soft smoothness of her breasts, which now bobbed free, moonlit and perfect. Cardero made a small sound of pleasure and kissed each pink, taut nipple once.

Then, without another word, he rose and took off his shirt, kicked off his boots, and discarded his trousers. He stood over Jessica Starbuck, naked and lean, his manhood evident, strong and ready.

She gave up trying to understand this man, to solve the puzzle of his character. She sat up and wrapped her arms around his thighs, drawing him to her, feeling his hands go to her shoulders.

Her own body was pulsing, growing damp, preparing itself. Her lips brushed Diego's inner thighs, her hands clenched his hard buttocks, and she lay back, her honey-blond hair tangled, veiling her face but not her smile.

Jessica kicked off her own boots, tugged her jeans down, and lay watching, just watching.

Cardero's eyes slowly swept over her, devouring every inch of smooth white flesh, of long, sleek thighs, of round, firm breasts, and of blond soft nest of hair.

Then he went down to her and his lips continued the examination, tasting her ears, her throat, breasts, and belly.

"Here," Jessie said, and she rolled slightly. An impatient hand reached, searching for and finding Cardero's long, solid shaft. She touched the head of it to her inner softness and sighed. She positioned him as she lay and rose to meet his entry. Her eyes were moonlit, her lips parted, slack, as Cardero inched ahead and slid into her moist depths.

She felt him tense, felt his hands. And she reached again, cupping his sack, holding him deep within her, keeping him motionless until she could stand it no longer, and she began to sway slowly against him, to work her body in small, demanding circles against him, feeling his movement deep inside where her own body, adjusting, wanting, had become utterly responsive.

She was wet with need and overcome by a sudden urge to slam herself against him, to twist and writhe and devour him. A small cry emerged from her throat and Cardero, stimulated by the sound, by the rush from Jessie's body, began to drive against her.

His hands were on her buttocks, his back was arched, his teeth set, as he throbbed within her, burying himself to the hilt, feeling the answering movements of her body, the hard, needful pitch and roll and thrust of her, hearing a second, joyous cry escape her lips.

Then Cardero could hold himself back no more and he finished with a series of long, jerking movements that brought a deep, racking, rushing climax.

He fell against Jessie, her arms wrapping around his neck, pulling his face down to meet her nearly savage kiss.

She continued to sway against him, small finishing movements that brought lingering satisfaction to her body, which was gradually cooling, gradually draining of need and tension.

Cardero was still against her, his soft breathing brushing against her throat. She hugged him and watched the stars. She tried not to think about what kind of man this was, this bandit, Diego Cardero.

She closed her eyes briefly, enjoying her body's warmth, its satisfaction. When she opened them again, a man with a rifle was standing over them.

Chapter 4

Carlos had an indescribably dirty leer on his crooked face. The rifle in his hands glinted dully in the moonlight. Cardero rolled over and sat up. He started to rise, but Carlos shoved him back.

"Damn you, Carlos."

"Shut up. I've got the gun. Why should you get all the fun, eh? It's my turn now."

Diego didn't answer. Instead, he launched himself at Carlos, a low growl rising from his throat as he clutched at the rifle in Carlos' hands.

Carlos was a little quicker. He stepped back and slapped out with the stock of his rifle. There was a sickening thud as the stock met Diego Cardero's jaw, and Diego rolled aside, holding his face and with his leg twitching.

"And now you lie back," Carlos told Jessie. "Now it is my turn, eh?"

Carlos dropped his pants as Jessie eased away. The bandit stood over her, rifle still in hands. "Hold still," he told her, "and do this my way."

There was a small, unidentifiable sound then, like a

cleaver cutting into meat. Carlos had been smiling; now he looked merely puzzled. He turned to look behind him and fell over dead, the arrow in his back snapping of as he hit the ground.

Diego had come to a little and he was in time to see Carlos fall. Someone moved on the rocks above them and the bandit reached for Carlos' rifle. From one knee he fired a shot, which whined off rock, singing into the night. The man, whoever it was, was gone.

"Get dressed quickly!" Diego said. "That shot will bring them."

"What are you going to do? What are you going to tell them?" Jessica wanted to know.

"Quickly, quickly, little one." Diego kissed her briefly and then was tugging his own clothing on. Already they could hear the excitement in the camp below, hear shouting and the rushing of feet.

Cardero was still tucking in his shirt when the bandits, fully armed and with Mono at their head, arrived.

"What happened? Who's that?"

"Carlos," Halcón said, crouching beside the body. He peered up curiously at Diego. "An arrow in the back."

"What is this, Diego?" Mono asked. "What's happened here?"

"I just arrived. I was going to relieve Carlos. He had brought the woman up here. I don't know what he thought he was going to do to her, though I have a good idea. Someone fired an arrow into Carlos' back. I was in time to get one shot off, but it missed."

"Yaquis?"

"One supposes."

"Damn him. He was supposed to be on watch. Instead, he fools with the woman. We could have all had our throats cut in our sleep. Stupid bastard," Mono said, and he kicked the dead body of Carlos. He looked around, eyes scouring the hills. "No one sleeps tonight. They're out there and we now know it. No one touches this woman again. Understand me? I'll find plenty of women for you, all you want. But later! Leave this one alone. Stupid bastard," he then repeated, looking down at Carlos. Mono had his foot cocked back as if to kick the body again, but he never followed through. Jessica guessed there was only so much fun even a man like Mono could have kicking corpses.

"Spread out. Find positions! Don't shoot each other," Mono shouted. Then he returned his attention to Jessica and Diego. "Take her back to camp. Tie her again. Watch her and the Chinaman."

"Yes, Mono."

Then the bandit chief turned and walked away without another word, apparently satisfied completely with Diego's explanation of the night's events.

There was another man there yet, one who perhaps wasn't wholly satisfied: Halcón who stood watching Diego for a long minute, his black eyes unreadable in the moonlight. He looked at Jessie and then at Diego, nodded as with satisfaction, and then started after Mono in a silent trot.

"He knows," Jessica said.

"He knows something. No matter. He was no friend of Carlos anyway."

"No." Jessie looked at Carlos' body and then at the cliff where the Indian who shot him had been. One Indian. One arrow. "Is that the way the Yaquis would attack?" she asked Diego.

"I don't know. Who knows? Why? What are you thinking, Jessica?"

She shook her head. "Nothing. That is, I don't know. Something doesn't ring true here. What, I don't know."

"What about me, Jessica?" Diego asked. "Do I ring true to you now?"

She looked into his smiling eyes and felt his arm around her shoulders. Again she shook her head. "No, darn you, you don't ring true, Diego Cardero. You don't at all."

Ki was worried by the time they returned. Relief washed over his face as he saw Jessica, saw that she was safe. Diego had done a good job tying Ki. His wrists were behind him as were his legs. A noose was around his neck and the rope from that led to his ankles. There was little Ki could do by way of movement without strangling himself.

"Sit down, Jessica," Diego said.

"You're not going to leave him like that?" Jessie asked with some heat.

"Not now, now that I am here." Diego produced a knife and with it he cut the noose free of Ki's throat. He proceeded to tie up Jessie firmly, but not tightly enough to cut off the circulation. "And now," Diego said, "I am myself going to do something I don't do often—try some of that tequila. Would either of you care to join me? No? Well, then, I drink alone. Oh"—he had started away, but now he halted and turned back—"please don't make me shoot you, Ki. Let us all sit quietly the rest of the night."

"Diego," Jessie said in a whisper, "you could let us go—now while only we three are here. Ride with us."

"No." Diego smiled. "You misunderstand me, Jessica Starbuck. I can hardly let you go. I am sorry."

After a little bow, he turned and walked away, Jessie's puzzled eyes following him.

"What happened up there?" Ki asked. He had to repeat the question before Jessica heard him. Briefly she told Ki about Carlos and the arrow. Ki listened silently and nodded when she was through.

"Was it a Yaqui, Ki?" Jessica asked. "They all seem to think it was."

"Perhaps," Ki said. "Perhaps it was, after all, a Yaqui who killed Carlos. Whoever it was, I would say that he has done the world a favor."

Diego Cardero was crouched near the dead fire, a rifle

across his knees and a tin cup in his hand. His eyes were still on Jessica and Ki.

"This one, Ki?" Jessie asked in a low voice. "What do you make of him?"

"This one," Ki answered, "is the dangerous one, more dangerous perhaps than Mono. Yes, this one is the one to be watched."

The silver moon passed overhead and died behind the white mountains. Nothing moved on the desert. An owl called from somewhere and a coyote answered with a mournful howl and then was silent. If the Yaquis were out there, it seemed they had withdrawn, biding their time.

With the first gray light, the bandits dragged themselves back into camp after a long, cold watch among the rocks. Mono was in a terrible mood.

"Let's go. Now. We ride while it's cool."

"Ride where?"

"San Ignacio. I want water, food, tequila. To hell with Don Alejandro. He can wait another day for his prizes here."

Diego Cardero looked somewhat refreshed, his clothing barely dusty and his sombrero square on his head. He came to Jessica and Ki and helped them to their feet, cutting their ankle bonds so that they could ride.

"Remember what I promised you," he said in a low voice to Jessie. "No harm will come to you."

"And just how," she asked while glancing at Mono, "can you promise that?"

"Remember," was all he said. Then Diego walked to where the horses were being saddled.

"What have you done to him?" Ki asked.

Jessica only shook her head. "I'm not sure. Have I done something to him, or has he done something to me? For some reason, Ki, I trust this man, this Diego Cardero."

"Feminine instinct?" Ki asked with a slight smile.

"Perhaps," she answered soberly.

Arturo was there with their horses. "Get on. No one's in any mood for talk."

Jessica swung aboard the horse and had her boots tied to the stirrups. Ki was again hitched to the saddlehorn. Then, with Arturo slashing at their horses' flanks, they started forward with a jerk and followed the line of bandits out of the white canyon, leaving the Yaquis and Carlos behind.

The sun rose fully an hour later, fiery red and already shooting fingers of light and heat. By ten, the heat was insufferable. Ki rode limply, trying to marshal his forces and at the same time give the impression that he was a beaten and exhausted man. Ki was an incredible physical specimen with ropy, lean muscles and with reactions far exceeding those of these bandits who were for the most part going to fat, soaked in liquor, dull, and sluggish.

There would be a time when Ki would have the chance, that single chance to strike, and he meant to be ready. In the meanwhile he did his best to look exhausted and dazed.

Jessica glanced at Ki, who now rode next to her, and she smiled inwardly, knowing what was going on in his cunning mind.

Sometime after noon Ki looked up and saw through the thin haze of heat and blowing sand a monument dark and wavering. He blinked twice and then recognized it for what it was, the tower of a mission church.

"Jessica," he said quietly.

She blinked and looked at him.

"Ahead. There's a town ahead. San Ignacio, I suppose."

She peered forward, her eyes narrowing. Then she, too, could make out the tower, the surrounding adobe buildings, and the dull color of the village trees.

"And what is Mono bringing to them?" she asked.

Ki looked at the bandit leader whose red eyes were shining with dark pleasure. He looked like the devil about to deliver hell to San Ignacio.

Maybe that was just what he was.

Chapter 5

San Ignacio was an ancient town founded in the seventeenth century by Franciscan friars who chose the site because of the water supply and because of the large Indian population who offered many souls for the friars' tending.

The church itself was vast compared to other local structures. A bell tower rose to a hundred feet or more. Seven bronze bells of varying sizes hung inertly there. There was a wall around the mission, but the huge wooden gates stood open, and inside the walls was a garden with much cactus, some climbing, deep purple bougainvillea, and a patch of tall, green corn.

The village was dusty and low and made of adobe bricks. As the bandits rode through the streets, windows were slammed shut. Children ran toward the willows along the edge of the town; the street was empty before they reached the village square where a trickle of a fountain filled an octagonal tile basin.

Jessica saw movement from the corner of her eye, and she looked around in time to see two peons, both men, running from a building to a nearby alley.

Mono drew his pistol and fired at their heels. Four

puffs of dust sprang up. One of the men fell and had to drag himself into an alley.

"Sheep!" Mono roared with laughter, ejecting the spent cartridges and reloading. He swung down, shouldered two of his men aside, and ducked his head into the fountain. He turned, wiped back his stringy black hair, and replaced his sombrero.

"Where are you, sheep? Where is everyone today, eh? Aren't you happy to see Mono has come back? Lock up your daughters, sheep!"

He laughed again, perched on the rim of the fountain, and stared at the empty streets.

"Leave Miguel here with the horses," he said. "Everyone else to the cantina!"

The bandits cheered and fired their pistols into the air. Diego Cardero stood aside with arms folded. "What about the prisoners, Mono?"

"Bring them along. We'll find a place to lock them up," the bandit leader said impatiently.

They tramped up the empty street. Rough hands shoved Ki along. Once he was tripped and yanked to his feet. The bandits' laughter was loud and approving; they were ready to let loose, to have some fun. Violent fun.

The cantina door was locked, but it didn't do the little proprietor any good. Mono's boot smashed at the door and it sprang open.

"Sanchez, Sanchez! Don't hide from me. It's your old friend Mono!"

The owner of the cantina appeared, small, subservient, and scared to death, his protuberant eyes goggling at Mono and his men.

Already Arturo and Miguel were behind the bar, grabbing tequila bottles from the shelves, tossing them to the other bandits.

Mono missed the first one they threw him, laughed as it crashed against the earth floor, and caught a second, raising it high in a mock toast.

The proprietor hadn't moved. He stood wringing his hands, watching in unhappy anticipation.

"You remember us, Sanchez?" Mono grabbed the little man by his shirt front and yanked him to him. "Eh? You remember Mono and Arturo? Halcón?"

"I remember you," Sanchez barely squeaked.

"Good. Then you know what we want: music, much to drink, food. Where is that fat wife of yours? Have her serve up food for us."

"Yes, Mono."

Mono lifted the little man to his toes, made a sound of disgust, and then pushed him away hard. Sanchez was hurled back into a heavy table, catching his spine on the corner of it.

"What's the Chinaman doing here still? I told you to lock him up somewhere."

"Yes, Mono. Sanchez," Arturo said, "give me the key to your storeroom; we have a use for it." He nodded at Ki.

"And the woman," Diego Cardero said. Mono turned to look at him, bottle to his lips.

Arturo started to take Jessie by the shoulder, but Mono said, "Let the woman stay. Maybe she will talk to Mono, eh? Maybe she will see that Mono is not such a bad fellow after all."

"Your order, Mono, was—" Diego began.

"My order was my order, Cardero! Now I change it. Leave the woman. Put her in a chair. Sanchez! Where are those lazy musicians of yours? Bring on the mariachi! We need music."

Jessie and Ki exchanged a helpless glance. Ki didn't like this much. The bandits were going to get drunk and they were going to get violent. He wanted Jessie out of their reach.

But no one had asked Ki what he wanted. Arturo shoved him forward across the packed dirt floor of the dark cantina and toward a narrow corridor behind the bar to the right. A harried Sanchez stood watching them, his mouth working without making a sound. As Arturo passed, he said, "And find that daughter of yours, Sanchez."

"She's out of town. Visiting her aunt in Dos Caballos."

"Find her. You're lying."

Sanchez could just stand there bewildered and deathly afraid. His head bobbed in a motion that was neither affirmative nor negative; it was just a helpless response to a command he was afraid to follow and terrified to reject.

Arturo rattled the keys he held, selected a heavy iron key, and moved on, still pushing Ki ahead of him. They stopped at a narrow door, which Ki inspected quickly, meticulously: Iron hinges on the outside were bolted through three inches of solid oak; the door was windowless, fitted well, and exceptionally solid.

Arturo opened the door and nodded. "Get in there."

Ki's eyes met those of the bandit. He stepped forward into the storeroom, and Arturo kicked him on the base of the spine, driving him into the room.

"Get in, I said. I haven't got time to fool with you Chinaman."

Ki lay sprawled on the floor, his back arched with pain and his mouth open in silent anguish. The door banged shut and was locked, and Ki came slowly to his feet, his eyes flashing angrily in the darkness.

He moved slowly around the storeroom, finding nothing of any use. There were no windows, no other door. There were no tools that might have been useful in working on the heavy iron hinges of the door. The ceiling was low and appeared solid.

Ki sat on his haunches near the door, hearing the savage laughter of the bandits, the crashing of glass, the flow of Spanish curses.

He sat there and he brooded and watched the darkness.

They had Jessica. They had her and Ki could not allow that. They would get drunk and then they would get crazy. They were a pack of savage dogs and deserved to be treated in the same way. Ki made his vow then: They would be killed. He would wait no longer. The war would begin.

Jessica Starbuck sat with her wrists tied in front of her, watching the bandits drink and grow wilder. How far would Mono let them go? As far as he had allowed them in Sonoita where a town had been destroyed, its women raped, its men murdered?

Mono had other objectives just now—getting Ki and Jessie to Don Alejandro, to the great hacienda where Kurt Brecht seemingly lived as a Mexican nobleman while he directed the cartel's slaving business.

But perhaps Mono wouldn't care much after a few bottles of tequila. Maybe a day or two wouldn't matter that much. So long as they had liquor and entertainment.

"Drink," Arturo said. He had slipped up beside Jessica Starbuck. Now he drew a chair next to hers and poured half a tumbler of tequila for her. His voice was a command, "Drink this, Señorita Starbuck."

"No," Jessie said calmly, though her heart was beginning to hammer. After Carlos, who was dead, and Mono himself, Arturo was the one she feared the most. There was something unstable in his eyes, as if lurking devils lived there.

"No, thank you."

"Drink when I tell you, *gringa,*" Arturo said, gripping Jessie's shoulder. Arturo's eyes had gotten darker, the devils seemed nearer to the surface. In his world, in Mono's world, a prisoner, especially a woman, did what she was told to do. "You heard me."

"Leave her alone, Arturo."

Arturo's head snapped around. Diego Cardero stood behind him, smiling. His thumbs were hooked into his black, cartridge-studded gunbelt—very casually his hands rested there, very close to his guns.

"Go away, Diego, this isn't your damned business."

"It sure is," Diego said as casually as before. "Mono said to watch her; I'm watching her."

"Watch her. What do I care? Why can't she take a drink?" Arturo asked.

"She doesn't want to," Diego said reasonably.

"I don't give a damn what she wants." Arturo flung his half-empty bottle of tequila against the adobe wall of the cantina; it shattered, showering a corner table with glass and liquor. No one so much as looked around.

"She doesn't want to drink," Diego repeated.

"It won't hurt her. I can't do anything to her that will lessen her worth. Don Alejandro will still pay if she's a little bit drunk, a little bit screwed, eh?"

"Go on," was all Diego Cardero said, tilting his head no more than an inch. There was menace in those two words. Arturo understood very well. Diego Cardero's own devils revealed themselves briefly in his liquid eyes. "Leave her alone now."

Arturo rose and for a minute Jessie thought there was going to be trouble as the lanky bandit stood poised before Diego Cardero, his hand near his own holstered Colt. After a long, taut minute, however, Arturo merely slunk away, glancing back like a dog, beaten and resentful.

Jessica Starbuck let out a breath of relief. "Thank you," she said to Diego.

The bandit just nodded, reversed a wooden chair, and sat down, arms folded on its back. "I told you nothing would happen to you."

"This time. What happens when they all get drunk? What happens if it's Mono who takes a notion? He wasn't talking about keeping me around for polite conversation, you know."

"I know." Diego Cardero lifted his eyes to where Mono stood, one arm around Halcón, the other hand holding a bottle of tequila. The level in that bottle, in all the bottles, was rapidly lowering. They were unpredictable, these men. They had killed, all of them; few of them seemed to have a fear of death themselves. Perhaps because their lives were so empty except for the violence and blood, they had no real love of life.

Mono led them because he was the most savage of all. He had protected Jessica so far, but that was merely a whim, or perhaps some echo of an admonition to be kind to women.

Mono did exactly as he wished, however, and when he was drunk, he wished to do evil. He had killed women before. He had killed his friends over a two-peso bet for the hell of it and stood over their bodies, mocking them and spitting on them.

"What the hell are you doing with these people, Diego?" Jessica asked.

"I told you, I am a bandit."

"That's even too dignified a word for what Mono and his men are. Coyotes . . . no, that's an insult to that animal, isn't it? Maybe there is no word to fit them."

"And me?" Diego asked with a bright smile.

"And you what?"

"Am I a thing to you, Jessica Starbuck?" the bandit asked.

"What you are, Diego, I still don't know. You have a chance to show me now, don't you?"

"To show you?" The smile was as bright as ever, but the eyes narrowed slightly.

"You could help Ki and me out of this."

"That is one thing I cannot do," Diego said. The smile faded now.

"But—"

"It is the one thing I cannot do, Jessica. I am sorry, believe me."

She looked into his eyes, her heart filled with fury.

She looked and the funny thing was she did believe him. She believed that he was sorry, believed that he wanted to help, believed he could not.

"All right," she said. "We know where we stand now."

Their eyes held for a minute longer and then Jessica heard the front door of the cantina open. A small boy in shabby clothing peered in and then raced away. Behind him came a three-man mariachi band. They wore black, and their jackets and sombreros were ornately decorated with gold thread.

They looked as if they belonged in prison stripes. They moved slowly, cautiously, into the cantina like convicts. They were scared stiff.

"Music!" Mono boomed. "Come in, come in *muchachos!* Sanchez, give these three crows tequila. Play, my friends, play!"

They played from a small platform, and although their fingers were lively and bright, their faces were frozen in petrified unease. They knew Mono too well.

Jessica remained in her chair, watching, listening to the drunken boasts and the apparently often repeated stories. Someone had had his throat cut; someone had had her skirts lifted and, while she was held down, raped by six of the bandits. An Indian slave had given them trouble and been set afire.

Diego was still there, sitting silently and watching.

"Bastard tried to cut me," Miguel was saying, "I guess we taught him. Painted him with pitch and stuck a torch to him . . . ran off across the desert like a great firefly until we shot him."

"Now," Jessica Starbuck said to Diego, "now, I think I would like just a little tequila."

From somewhere in the back Arturo appeared, dragging someone behind him.

She was young and had dark eyes and full breasts. She wore a striped skirt and a white blouse that accented smooth dark shoulders.

"Maria!" Sanchez shouted. The cantina owner leaned against the bar rigidly like a man suffering apoplexy.

"Your daughter is back," Arturo said triumphantly. "Back so soon from Dos Caballos and visiting her aunt. Now she can visit with us, no? Visit with Arturo and his friends and join the party."

Sanchez shook his head heavily, despairingly. The girl was fiery and strong. Twisting free of Arturo's grip, she slapped away his hands. When he caught her by the wrist, she sunk her teeth into his arm, and the bandit yelped in pain. Mono and the others laughed, but there was no amusement in Arturo's eyes. He slapped the girl viciously, and she sat down hard on the floor, blood trickling from her mouth and staining her white blouse crimson.

"Bastard," she snarled, "filthy *cabrón*."

Arturo drew back his boot as if he were set to kick her, but Diego said sharply, "No!"

Arturo's eyes shifted to Diego, those devil-filled eyes that now were killing eyes.

"Don't tell me what to do, Cardero," Arturo said. "You stood against me once today already. Don't tell me what to do about this little slut. I will kick her teeth in if I wish and you will say nothing . . . or you will die."

Diego's hands slowly lowered to be nearer his guns. Arturo, standing over the girl who sat spraddle-legged on the floor, turned slightly to face Diego. It took Mono to break it up.

"Come on, Arturo!" the bearded giant shouted. "Drink with us. If you kick the girl's teeth out, she will not look so beautiful, eh? Not look like something a man would want to use. Musicians, what are you standing around for? Play for us! Now!"

Mono drew one of his own pistols, fired into the wall beside the bandstand, and laughed uproariously as the mariachis scrambled for their instruments and began frantically and unhappily to play a bright tune.

Arturo turned away from Diego, taking a last warning

glance at the tall man. The girl, Maria, still sat on the floor, her lips moving in a soundless curse until Diego helped her up.

She slapped his hands away as well and went behind the bar to help her father serve the thirsty *bandidos*. Outside somewhere a shot was fired and a gleeful yell went up. Mono, staggering slightly now, laughed again and called for another bottle.

Jessica Starbuck sat in a hard wooden chair, watching. It was going to be a long, long night.

Chapter 6

The night passed slowly, painfully. Ki glowered at the darkness, needing to fight back against it. Beyond the door, the drunken celebration continued.

Ki had examined the room he was locked in, looking for some way out. There was none—none but the heavy door that was barred shut. Now there was nothing left to do but sit and wait—wait for Mono and his men to finish their drinking, gambling, and fighting.

Then perhaps someone would decide it was too much trouble after all to watch Ki and cut his head off. And Jessica—that was the part that hurt, that caused a knot of anguish to build in Ki's stomach. She was out there with that mob of cutthroats.

Footsteps, light and rapid, sounded beyond the door and Ki's eyes lifted. He moved to the wall near the door and waited, his body tensing. His wrists were still tied, but his hands were still effective weapons. He weighed his chances quickly and decided he had no real hope of making an escape. Slowly he let his body relax.

The door swung open and Ki stepped back.

The woman with the tray entered and Ki blinked in

surprise. Young, darkly beautiful with black eyes, full breasts, and a wide slash of a mouth, she entered the dark room, looking around. Behind her in the lamplit corridor, Halcón stood with a rifle.

It was the Indian who spoke. "Better eat. Mono still wants you alive."

Halcón appeared indifferent to Ki's life or death. The girl had moved across the room, head down, to place the tray with its steaming frijoles, tortillas, and rice on the low shelf against the wall.

She passed Ki again, her dark eyes lifting to his and briefly sharing Ki's anger. Then she walked out, head down once more. Halcón kicked the door shut and the darkness returned. Ki heard the footsteps receding and he walked to the tray of food.

He ate without appetite, stared at the gloom surrounding him, and let his thoughts run in endless futile circles. There was no escape. None.

In the cantina the band played on. They had been at it for four hours, their fingers cramped and their voices now hoarse. Mono strode about the cantina, kicking over tables and shouting at the ceiling, his eyes red and glazed.

Jessica Starbuck sat alone. Now and then her eyes met Diego's, but they communicated nothing, nothing but vague contempt for this man who had promised no harm would come to her but had said that he could not help her escape. Jessica made no sense out of that, and it angered her, angered her almost as much as the knowledge that she still liked this man, wanted him.

"I want a woman!" It was Arturo who suddenly shouted this in a voice audible above the crash of tables and the mariachi band.

"Go get one." Miguel, boots propped up on a table, encouraged him. "And bring me one as well."

"Don't think I won't. Where the hell's Sanchez's daughter?"

Behind the counter, Sanchez winced visibly and paled.

"Gone," Sanchez said, but no one seemed to hear him.

"Come on." Miguel got to his feet unsteadily. His sombrero hung by its string down his back. His crossed pistols rode low on his thighs. "Let's go out and get some women."

"Plenty of them," the bandit named José shouted.

Mono said nothing. He watched his men without apparent interest. They wanted women; let them have them. Diego was smiling and smoking a cigar, his long legs crossed. Jessica could have killed him at that moment.

Miguel, José, and Arturo eventually staggered out the door to catcalls and encouragement from the other *bandidos*. The green cantina door stood open. Smoke seeped out into the night. Jessica saw the three men stumble toward the street and then they were gone.

Two bandits had begun a knife-throwing contest. Jessica watched them, listened to them, and watched the open door. She thought of making a desperate dash for it, but even as she thought that, she recognized the sheer futility of it. Eight *bandidos* remained in the cantina and there was just no way she was going to make it to the door and freedom.

"Oh, Ki," she said under her breath, "we've really gotten ourselves into it this time."

The noise and roughhousing went on. One of the bandits was stabbed in the hand, and Mono broke that skirmish up before it got deadly.

Miguel was back within a half hour. He was dragging someone behind him—a petrified, struggling girl of fifteen or so, her eyes wild with terror. Miguel was laughing.

"Here's one at least."

"Not quite ripe, is she?"

Miguel's hands ran across the girl's body and he smiled nastily. "She's ripe. She's ready."

"Leave her alone." The voice was Jessica's, sounding

hoarse and furious. Miguel turned to look at her, mock fear on his dark face.

"Oh, so now the *gringa* shows fire, too."

Miguel started toward her. There was no telling what his intentions were, but Diego Cardero halted him. He simply recrossed his legs, rested his hand near his side-arm, and shook his head. Miguel started to snarl something, grinned instead, and said to the girl, "Come on, little one, let's see if you can dance."

Mono applauded that idea. "Dance! By all means! Mariachis, why have you stopped playing? The little one here wants to dance for us."

The girl was shoved to the center of the cantina floor. Chairs and tables were thrown aside for her, clearing an area.

She stood immobilized, her lips trembling as the band began to play.

"Well, dance, damn you!" Miguel shouted and the girl began to stamp her feet, to move around the floor, her face an iron mask, her hands clapping rhythmically.

"Yes, yes!" It was Arturo who did the shouting from the doorway. He and José had returned with a prize of their own, a middle-aged woman in black. She had a little too much weight, but there was still enough youth packed into her body to interest the *bandidos*. She had worn her hair pinned up, but now it hung in strands on one side. The top of her dress had been ripped open. There were long red scratches on the side of Arturo's face.

"You dance too, fat one."

"You kiss the devil!" she spat.

"Dance or go outside with me again," Arturo said with a slow, leering grin.

"Pigs," the older woman said, "all of you are pigs."

But she went to the center of the floor and began a slow defiant dance.

The musicians had just finished the first number when

the door to the cantina burst open. A peon, a small man with a wilted straw sombrero and a face as dark as mahogany, stepped inside.

"My wife," he said very slowly, very softly.

Mono's massive head slowly turned toward the little man. There was wine and tequila in Mono's tangled beard. His eyes glittered a little. Jessica felt her hands tighten on the arms of the chair.

"Señor?" Mono inquired softly.

"That is my wife, *señor,"* the little man said. The older woman had started forward toward him, but Arturo had yanked her back roughly.

"Is it now? Is she a good wife?"

"Yes, she is a good wife."

"Good to take to bed?" Mono asked with a casual gesture.

"She is a good woman. This is not the place for her."

"You know who I am?" Mono asked.

"I know who you are, Mono. Everyone in San Ignacio knows who you are."

"Bueno." Mono smiled indulgently. "Then tell the devil hello for me."

His gun had been on his lap. Now he aimed and fired. Thunder filled the room as Mono's Colt spat flame. The bullet hit the peon in the face, toppling him and spattering the wall behind him with blood. The woman screamed. Arturo laughed out loud at Mono's little joke.

"You bastards," Jessica said. Whether they heard her or not, no one looked at her—no one but Diego Cardero who was still smoking, still appearing unruffled by any of this. Jessica glanced at him once, her eyes cutting, and then she turned her head away.

"Get that thing out of here," Mono commanded. "And dance! Who told you to stop dancing?" He fired again, a bullet punching through the fine polished wood of a guitar. "Sing, dance, drink. The night is young and we mean to fill it with pleasure!"

The sound of the shot had reached into Ki's cell. His head came up, his mind filling with all sorts of possibilities as to the shot's meaning. There had been other random shots throughout the evening, but this one had somehow sounded different. It had carried an echo of death.

Ki rose and paced the room again. He felt helpless and he despised the feeling. He was a man who was used to directing the course of his own fate with his two good hands and his mind. This, not seeing, not knowing, not having any useful course of action, was nearly insufferable.

Outside the door Ki heard a quick scuffling sound, a muted groan. He spun that way, waiting, expecting anything but what he saw next.

The door opened slowly and the woman named Maria and who had brought his food stood there, backlighted by the lantern. Behind her on the floor lay Halcón.

"Hurry," she said impatiently. She gestured toward the corridor, and Ki, ready to take almost any chance no matter how small, followed her quickly.

He stepped over Halcón who lay still, a huge iron skillet beside him on the floor, and followed the girl down the corridor in the opposite direction from the cantina.

The girl had Halcón's pistol in her hand. She slipped it to Ki who tucked it away almost carelessly behind his belt. "Here," she hissed.

As Ki waited, she opened a back door, peered out into the night, and nodded her head. Ki went after her into the starlit darkness beyond the door. Muffled curses, shouts, whistles, music followed them and then were shut off as the door closed.

"Run now," Maria whispered.

"No." Ki stood before the much shorter young woman, rubbing his wrists.

"Run or they will kill you. I intend to run."

"You should," Ki responded. "Take this pistol if you want it."

"You need a weapon."

Ki replied, "I am not unarmed," and the woman just stared up at him, wondering if he was perhaps a madman the outlaws had captured for some reason she could only guess at.

"I don't have a horse to give you—" she began to say.

"I thank you for what you have already done, but I don't need a horse just now."

The woman didn't understand at first. Then she did. "The girl inside, the blond *gringa?* You mean to try to save her as well?"

"Yes," Ki answered quietly. "I mean to save her as well."

"Impossible! Mad one, that cannot be done. If it could, don't you think I would do it?" There was fire in the woman's eyes, bright and defiant. Ki smiled gently.

"Run. They will know who struck Halcón."

"You can't go back there."

"I can try," Ki answered.

"And defeat Mono and all his thugs? And rescue the *gringa?* And maybe the other captive women, the two they are using for dancing? Later they will have other uses for them. I know. Mono has been here before. One woman he drove mad. She was a woman of the church and Mono raped her. He raped her in front of all of his men and laughed when the woman screamed and cried and thrashed. My father saw it. He also saw a chance and told me to run. Now!"

"Then run," Ki repeated very quietly.

Before the woman could respond, the back door of the cantina burst open. Miguel, rifle in hands, charged out into the night.

He was looking for Ki apparently, looking for whoever had slugged Halcón, but he came out too quickly, not giving his eyes time to adjust to the darkness, not giving himself enough time to find his enemy before he ran right into him.

There was no hesitation at all in Ki's movements. He spun the girl away from him, crouched, and as the startled Miguel brought his rifle to his shoulder, Ki sprang from the earth, his foot striking out at Miguel's throat.

The leaping kick nearly decapitated Miguel as Ki's foot caught the bandit under the chin, crushing cartilage and snapping his head back. Miguel's eyes bugged out of his head; a strangled cry gurgled through his broken throat. Ki landed softly and turned, his hands poised, but already he knew he would not have to strike at Miguel again. The man was dead, lying still and dark in the wedge of light that bled out into the alley from the cantina.

Softly Ki closed the door, glancing at Maria who had her fingers to her lips. "I never saw—" she began to say, but Ki took her hand and quieted her.

"Not now. Come. There will be others."

"You will run away with me?"

"For now I will run. Get moving now; there will be more."

"My father's house . . ." she said breathlessly as they started at a trot up the darkened alley behind the cantina.

"That is the first place they would look," Ki said. "There must be another place, a place the *bandidos* would know nothing about, a place you played in when you were a little girl, perhaps."

"There is." Maria panted. "I know a place. Just a goatherd's shack—back among the willow trees on an island in the river. The goatherd has been dead many years."

"All right. That'll have to do," Ki said. Behind him there were shouts and curses from the cantina. They had found Miguel. "Hurry, Maria. Hurry now or we'll never see morning."

They crossed the plaza, Ki moving in a crouch, and

ran on past the closed church. The river ahead of them gleamed dully and wound through the willows like a blue satin ribbon.

They stopped at the bank of the river, Maria holding her breast, breathing raggedly.

"Which way now?" Ki asked, and she pointed one finger.

"We wade the river. It's very shallow. The island . . ." She paused for breath. "When the goatherd lived there, it wasn't an island, but the river has changed its course."

They walked into the water, which rose to Ki's knees and slogged across toward the island. An owl dipped low and then veered away sharply as Ki and Maria waded past the center of the stream and worked toward the far beach.

Ki glanced back once and saw no pursuit, but there would be some—if not tonight when the drinking seemed momentarily more important, then at first light. Ki could not be allowed to escape. He had killed one of their own.

And he was still worth something. There was a cartel bounty on him, and Mono, mad as he was, wouldn't be willing to throw that away.

Nor would he now be willing to take Ki to the Don Alejandro alive—not when Ki's severed head would serve just as well.

They reached the far bank, which was muddy and steeply sloped, and clambered up and into the willows, using the tangled roots projecting from the bank.

Into the willows they moved slowly, fighting off the brush and the swarms of mosquitoes. Maria lost her way, found it, lost it again, and then they changed directions until the willows suddenly parted. In a small, well-concealed clearing, they came upon the old goatherd's shack.

It was of bark and willow branches, but the door was made from sturdy pine planks and showed little signs of rot or time's depredations.

Ki jiggled the door and got it to open on its ancient hinges. Inside it was dark, still, smelling of age. Something scuttled away in the darkness.

As their eyes adjusted, they could see the ancient bed made of leather straps tacked to a framework of two-by-fours, a tilting table, and two wooden chairs. Ki crossed the room, opened a window, and stood looking out and listening for a long while.

Maria watched him. He stood silhouetted before the stars, tall and handsome and competent. She felt a small stirring in her belly and was surprised by it.

"Are they coming?" she asked.

"I don't see anyone. I'll stand watch outside, though. I don't think anyone can cross the river without me hearing them."

Maria just nodded. She looked to the bed. Ki followed her eyes there. By the starlight he could make out her weary expression, the fine structure of her facial bones, and the swell and thrust of her young, ripe breasts. Her skirt was soaked through, her shoes wet.

"Lie down," Ki told her. "Take off your skirt before you catch a chill. I'll be outside. Don't worry, I won't bother you."

Maria started to say something in answer and failed to accomplish it. She poked around and found an old blanket rolled up under the bed. When she shook it, a few moths and a cloud of dust flew out, but it would keep the chill away through the night.

Ki had gone to the door, and with a last backward glance, he went out to watch and wait. He had spent much time doing just that—watching and waiting—for Ki was a warrior and much of a warrior's time is filled with waiting.

The stars were full and bright. The willows stood as dark, slowly shifting creatures responding to the whims of the night breeze. Downstream frogs in abundance chorused. If anyone were coming that way, the frogs would stop abruptly and so would the crickets that chirped all around Ki as he sat quietly, feeling the night.

For hours he watched, barely moving, until he heard the door open behind him, heard the soft footsteps, felt the gentle hand fall onto his shoulder.

"I am frightened," Maria said. "It's dark and cool, and I'm alone. Come in with me."

★

Chapter 7

Ki turned and rose slowly. The night air was cool, the woman before him young and beautiful. There was something in her soft, dark eyes beyond the obvious fear and uncertainty. Perhaps it was nothing more than the timeless longing of a woman for a man, a man strong, protective, and capable of keeping away hunger, danger, and the night.

"Come inside with me," Maria said again, and her small hand closed around Ki's.

Ki looked into her eyes once more and then he nodded. Death was roaming the streets of San Ignacio and the desert beyond, but he could do nothing about that just now. What he could do was drive the fear out of a woman's heart for just a little while and lose himself in the forgetfulness of lovemaking.

She had made the little bed neatly. Inside she stopped, turned hesitantly, and kissed Ki's lips. Then she slipped from the white chemise she wore and stood before him naked and lovely in the starlight.

Ki touched her with his eyes before his hands so much as stretched out to her. He looked at the sleek lines of her neck and her full, slightly parted lips. He let his gaze drop to her dark-nippled, full breasts and then to the slender waist and the flaring, womanly hips.

He stepped to her and his hands went around her waist, his fingers tracing patterns across her bare, smooth back and then dropping to her ass, so full and solid and sheathed by flawless honey skin.

He kissed her and drew her closer, feeling her shudder. Then with a smile he stepped away, just studying her for a moment. She bowed her head, leaning against Ki, her fingers going to the buttons of his shirt, unfastening them as her lips found his chest. She tasted the small dark nipples and then found his navel, which her tongue explored as Ki's hands rested on her shoulders.

Maria lay back on the bed and watched Ki kick off his soft shoes and remove his trousers. She caught her breath when she saw him standing naked before her, his manhood erect and proud. Ki went to her and she sat on the edge of the bed, one hand encasing his erection, stroking it gently. Her thumb moved across the tender head of it. Her other hand clenched his buttocks and drew him nearer. Her cheek was against his belly; her hair soft and dark was loose and pleasant against Ki's eager flesh.

"Come down to me," Maria said. "Come down and show me how to make love to you."

She lay back, her eyes bright, her skin smooth and glossed by starlight. Ki knelt, kissing her soft inner thighs. He felt the quivering there as his fingers found her core and searched her soft inner flesh.

Ki kissed her belly, found her breasts with his lips, and moved on top of her, his body seeming weightless but strong, very strong.

Maria closed her eyes partly, her mouth opened to meet Ki's gentle, searching kiss. She responded eagerly, arching her back. Her tongue tasted Ki's lips as he positioned himself, feeling the heat from her body, the urging of her kisses.

Maria reached down, found his shaft, toyed with it, her legs spreading slightly and then lifting as she wriggled onto him. Her breath began to come in short gasps, her body responding with a rush of liquid.

Ki drew her to the side of the bed without losing her. He knelt on the floor beside the bed as Maria locked her legs around his waist, her arms around his shoulders. Her full, round breasts flattened themselves against his chest.

Ki stroked the woman with his knowing hands, touching her ears, tracing them, moving slowly across the nape of her neck to her spine where his fingers trailed downward skillfully. Then with a sudden, powerful grip, he clutched at her ass with both hands and lifted her onto him as Maria gasped.

Ki reached beneath her, spreading her still more, stroking her, feeling the sweet dampness there, feeling the pulsing of Maria's body, the increasing urgency of her kisses, her warm, moist breath against his cheek and ear.

Maria's legs, locked around his waist, clenched him as if she would squeeze him in half. Ki paid no attention to that. He had begun to move against her—slowly, deftly, letting his body find each fold and tender button of Maria's trembling body.

He held her to him, looking into her eyes, eyes that revealed the depth of her pleasure.

"Harder, Ki. Please. Now a little slower."

Ki smiled and did as she asked, sometimes plunging his shaft into the hilt and lifting her from the edge of the bed with the power of his strokes. At other times he moved gently, almost teasingly, with slow care, driving inward a bare inch at a time.

Maria made small sounds deep in her throat, small hungry sounds. She still spoke to Ki, but the words made no sense. Half of them were in Spanish, half in the language of passion.

Then her body spoke very clearly as she, arching her back and reaching down with one hand to find where Ki entered her, trembled and let loose a torrent. Maria cried out loudly, bit at her wrist, and settled to a deep, constant trembling.

Now Ki began to sway in rhythm, a slow, deeply thrusting rhythm that caused his own thighs to tremble, that lifted his own desire to need, that brought his need to a gushing climax.

Maria cried out again with pleasured satisfaction and held Ki's shaft as he finished, throbbing and spasming within her.

"Lie with me," she said finally, and shaking, she pulled herself back onto the bed. Ki followed without slipping from her. He followed and lay beside her, letting her touch his shoulders, chest, and hard thighs with a kind of primitive wonder until the Mexican girl fell off to a contented sleep, her mouth slightly parted to reveal her teeth. Her long lashes now and then moved and once opened to reveal dark, deeply satisfied eyes.

Ki let her fall into a sound, lasting sleep and then he rose. The *bandidos* were still out there somewhere and he couldn't afford the luxury of a night's sleep. He went out quietly, stood beneath the stars, watched the silky river run, and listened to the night sounds of insects and frogs and night predators.

They still had Jessica Starbuck.

They had her and that could not be allowed. Ki frowned. He had effected his own escape, but that might or might not have been to Jessie's advantage. Would they now bind her more tightly, increase the guard, chain her . . . or worse?

The head of Jessica Starbuck would still bring a huge reward from the cartel, from Don Alejandro as Kurt Brecht had taken to calling himself.

Something moved in the darkness and Ki crouched, his muscles bunching, his hands positioning themselves. The night held something, someone. Ki could feel it, but he could see nothing. The frogs still croaked in the cattails; the crickets still chirped as if whatever was out there moved invisibly, without a whisper of sound.

The feeling lingered for a time and then passed and Ki gradually relaxed. For another three hours he kept his silent watch. An hour or so before dawn, Maria, yawning, came to the door of the goatherd's shack. She came to him, put her arms around his waist, and rested her head on his chest.

"Is everything all right?" she asked.

"I think so. Yes." Ki didn't explain about the silent thing in the willows.

"What will you do now?" Maria's dark questioning eyes met Ki's.

"I will free Jessica Starbuck," Ki answered. He shrugged and kissed Maria's forehead lightly.

She didn't smile in answer. "How, Ki?" she asked. "How do you plan to free her from Mono's *bandidos?"*

"Now," Ki replied, "you have asked the difficult question. I don't know how I will do it."

"If I can help you . . ."

"You can't go back into San Ignacio, not now. They know you helped me."

Maria's temper flared briefly. "Do you think I am a coward, Ki?"

"No, I think nothing of the sort."

"Then I will help you."

Ki held her for a minute. The air was damp and cool, the river a whispering thing moving past them. To the East the sky was graying. Birds were beginning to stir in the willows.

"We have to find out what they are doing, where they have Jessica," Ki said thinking out loud.

"It will be daylight soon."

"That might be a disadvantage. On the other hand, the nearer it gets to dawn the more the *bandidos* will have drunk and the more likely they will be to fall asleep or at least be off their guard."

"I have many friends and family in San Ignacio," Maria said. "Some of them might help."

"I don't want help just now."

"Maybe you need some," Maria said. She bit her lip thoughtfully.

"You have something in mind?" Ki asked.

"Clothing. What you wear is too obvious. A peon costume, a serape. You are just dark enough if someone doesn't look too closely."

The woman was right. It wasn't a bad idea at all to try disguising Ki. The moment he was spotted, Mono's people would try to kill him. Perhaps the moment of recognition could be delayed with a disguise.

"My cousin Fernando is not quite as tall as you, but nearly. And, he is a barber," Maria said with sudden inspiration.

Ki frowned. "What has that to do with this?"

"You will see. Let's go now. Fernando is on the far side of town. We can follow the river without being seen."

Ki was dubious, but he had no better idea. He was ready to accept any help that was offered just now.

They moved along the bank as the first colors of sunrise began to streak the sky. The river absorbed the colors and reflected them darkly. Ki stopped suddenly.

"What is it?" Maria asked, her eyes widening. She crouched a little as Ki was doing and looked around.

"Just this." Ki pointed it out. A footprint in the sand, a very fresh footprint. It had to have been made during the night. "So," Ki said, "he is not a phantom after all."

"What are you saying, Ki?" Maria asked nervously.

"What does this mean? Does Mono know where we are?"

"No, this was not one of Mono's *bandidos*. You see, this was made by a moccasin."

"There are no Indians around here," the Mexican girl said.

"There is," Ki corrected, "at least one." One who had come a long way, following them from the Cañon del Dios in Arizona, one who had killed Carlos back at Tinaja Caliente. Ki stood and looked around carefully, his eyes—eyes used to searching, to careful watching—still failing to find anyone, anything. There was only the single track in the sand as if in a careless moment this phantom had become a creature of flesh, blood, and bone and formed it in his passing.

"I don't like this, Ki," Maria said. She hunched her shoulders as if a sudden chill had crept over her.

"No," Ki answered, "neither do I. Let's go on to your cousin's house before the sun rises."

They went on, hurriedly now, Ki with the strange feeling that there were eyes watching his back, dark eyes that waited, wanting what?

The golden rim of the sun had crept above the dark line of the desert horizon before they reached Fernando's house.

It was a small adobe with a red tile roof, shuttered windows, and a door which was firmly barred. It might have been abandoned, but Ki could smell cooking within the house. Maria pounded on the door with the side of her fist.

"Fernando, Alicia! Open the door. It's me, Maria Sanchez."

"Who is that with you?" a voice answered after a long interval.

"A friend."

"What friend?" the challenging male voice wanted to know.

"Someone you don't know, Fernando. I'll explain inside, but for the sake of Our Lady, let us in now, please!"

The door opened hesitantly and then swung wide. Maria hurried inside, Ki on her heels. A tall Mexican in longjohns waited, watching. Five sets of dark, children's eyes watched from across the room where Fernando's children clustered around the large, sheltering figure of his wife.

"Now what is this? *Madre de Dios,"* Fernando said, running a hand across his rumpled hair. "To come to a man's house at this time of the morning at a time like this!"

"We need your help, Fernando," Maria said.

"My help? You can't stay here. No, if Mono—"

"We don't want to stay," Maria said a little scornfully. "My friend Ki here is going to fight Mono and you will help him."

"Me fight Mono!" Fernando made violently negative gestures with his hands. "No, I have the children, I have my wife—"

"She doesn't mean that I want you actually to fight the *bandidos,"* Ki said. Maria had begun to enjoy taunting her cousin. "She only wants you to lend me some clothes."

"And a little something else," Maria said. "Anyway, why won't you fight? You men of San Ignacio!" she spat. "Whose town is this anyway, yours or Mono's?"

"It is ours when Mono is away," Fernando said. "But when he comes, it is his. Everything is his. He comes, takes what he wants, does what he wants, and then after a little while, if we are patient, he goes away."

"Leaving pain and destruction behind."

"He breaks a few things. Steals a little—"

"Beats a few men, kills some, rapes your wives and your daughters!" Maria went on with savage mockery.

"We survive!" Fernando said, growing angry now. "Mono is a killer, a pig. He has killed many men; all of them have. They have destroyed towns when they were not pleased. What good does it do my children to have their house burned down around them, to have their father killed, to have the crops destroyed?"

Ki said, "Maria, we have business."

"Yes." Maria looked at her cousin for a long while. Her expression softened and at last she smiled, hugging Fernando. "I am sorry. Everything is so hard. You are doing the right thing."

"I am doing all I can," Fernando said, still defensive.

"Yes," Maria replied. "Now do one more thing. Let this man Ki wear some of your clothes."

Fernando was reluctant to do even that it seemed, but under Maria's scathing gaze he agreed. The peon costume nearly fit Ki, though it was a bit short all around. With a pair of sandals and a red and black serape, Ki's disguise was complete.

Or so he thought. Maria had other ideas. *"Bueno,"* she said, looking Ki up and down. "Now we go into Fernando's shop, eh?"

"My shop, but why?" Fernando asked.

"Come on, come on. Also, find a sombrero, Alicia, *por favor."* She took Ki by the arm and guided him to the inner door, which Fernando, muttering, opened and entered. Beyond was the barber shop. Maria, looking around, spied the box where the sweepings were kept. She fished around, found what she wanted as the two men exchanged an uneasy glance, and turned with her trophy.

"Now," she said, holding up a hank of dark hair, "a little resin . . ." She walked to Ki, held the clippings up under his nose, and nodded. "It will do for a mustache. After it is stuck on, Fernando will trim it for you."

Ki didn't think much of the idea, but he had to admit after the hair was gummed on and trimmed that it disguised him effectively.

"This isn't going to come off, is it?" Ki asked Fernando, who was giving the mustache a final snip.

"You will be lucky, *señor,*" the barber said, "if that ever comes off your lip."

Maria stood watching, arms folded beneath her breasts and quite pleased with herself.

Ki examined himself again in a hand mirror Fernando gave him, shook his head, and said, "And now the simple part is over. Now it is up to me to use this disguise."

"Señor," Fernando said, "you are really going to fight Mono?"

"I hope not," Ki said honestly. "I hope I do not have to fight anyone to free my friend Jessica Starbuck. There are too many of them and they're too eager to kill. But I will get her out of there—no matter what it takes."

Fernando put his scissors and mirror away, shaking his head in wonder. There are many madmen in this world. It seemed that he had just met one, for any man who would try to stand against Mono the killer was mad.

"Now," Ki said, standing and placing the straw sombrero on his head, "we will see exactly what can be done." Ki started toward the door then, and in the mirror he saw Fernando silently cross himself.

A last prayer for a madman.

Chapter 8

The sun was bright, the pueblo still and apparently empty, though Ki knew all of the houses were filled with people like Fernando and Alicia, hiding fearfully, waiting, and praying that the bandits would ride out, firing a few last shots in the air, leaving the town to its peace.

Ki asked, "Who cleans up your father's cantina?"

"What?" Maria blinked, not understanding the question's relevance at first. Then she did understand and she replied, "My uncle, Natividad. But he will not go there today. No one would with Mono and his men there."

That wasn't exactly true, for there was at least one man in San Ignacio who would dare that task.

"Will your father give me away?"

Maria thought. "He is not a brave man, but, no, I don't think he will give you away. Ki," she said, "this is not a good plan. If you are recognized, they will certainly kill you. There must be another way to do this thing."

"Yes?" Ki waited for a suggestion that made sense, but there was nothing Maria could say; there was no other way but to walk right in there and hope for the opportunity to get Jessie away from those killers.

"That's what I thought," Ki said. "You go on back to the shack or wherever you think you will be safest."

"The mission church," she replied without hesitation. "They will not find me there."

"All right. Maria . . ." Ki's eloquence deserted him. What could he say when he didn't know if he would see her again, when he didn't know if he would survive this day. She went to tiptoes and kissed him and then spun away almost in anger, walking toward the distant, high-walled mission church.

Ki watched her for a moment. Then resolutely tugging his sombrero lower and hunching his back to make himself appear smaller, less athletic, he shuffled off through the empty, dusty streets of San Ignacio toward the cantina.

He approached through the back alley. There was no one on the streets at all. A yellow dog, rail thin, watched Ki pass his resting place in the shade; otherwise Ki didn't see a living thing.

Until he saw Arturo.

The bandit was perched on a barrel, dark sombrero worn over his eyes and rifle across his knees. Ki slowed his pulse and continued on, shuffling to where the *bandido* sat.

"What do you want, dog?" Arturo growled.

"To clean up, *señor,* to sweep as I always do."

Arturo tipped his hat back a little and with red, glassy eyes peered at the narrow, hunched peon before him. "All right," he said at last, "but be careful you don't wake anyone up. Mono is in there asleep. You know Mono, don't you, dog?"

"Sí, señor."

"If you wake Mono up, maybe he'll clip your *huevos* off for you. Understand me?"

"Yes, I understand. Very quiet—but I must sweep."

Arturo grunted something, pulled his hat down again, and apparently went to sleep himself as Ki entered the back door, his rope-soled sandals shuffling along the corridor.

Sanchez, exhausted from the night's work and the tension, was behind the counter on a stool, his head resting on his arms. His head came up quickly, his eyes registering confusion.

"Who . . . ?"

"It is only me, Natividad," Ki said. "Come to sweep up."

Sanchez's eyes narrowed. Something about this stranger registered in the back of his mind, but Sanchez couldn't put his finger on just what it was. Sanchez simply remained silent rather than stir up the bandits in any way. He watched without comment as the man who was pretending to be Natividad found a broom and began to work among the tables where the bandits sprawled, reeking of sour liquor and tobacco, of sweat and gun-powder.

Mono's eyes blinked open suddenly and the bandit chief glowered at Ki. Ki saw Mono's body tense, saw his meaty hand drop toward his gun butt. It was over. The bandit king was going to kill him, carry his severed head off to the cartel, and have his way with Jessica Starbuck.

But it didn't happen that way. Mono didn't recognize Ki any more than Sanchez did. He opened his bleary eyes, saw a peon sweeping the floor of the saloon, and closed his eyes again, letting his huge hand drop away from the butt of his Colt.

Ki worked silently among the drunk, sleeping outlaws. His eyes measured each man, noted his position, and his sweeping took him closer and closer to the blond woman dozing in a corner chair.

Ki looked around again, noticing that Diego Cardero was not around. With his broom he nudged the leg of Jessie's chair, then nudged it again, harder yet.

Her green eyes popped open.

Maybe Sanchez and Mono didn't recognize Ki, but Jessica Starbuck had been long on the trail with this man, this Ki, and she knew him instantly. Her lips parted automatically to speak, but she was awake enough to clamp them shut again.

Her hands were tied, but her ankles were not. Looking around slowly, she saw that the outlaws still slept, except possibly for the guard out front and the one in the back alley.

Ki was there and wonderfully alert. He had pasted on a mustache and borrowed some clothing, but it was Ki and Jessie's heart lifted slightly, suddenly, as Ki nodded toward the back corridor.

They were going to try it. They were going to try to make their escape from under the guns of Mono and his band of criminals. They had no weapons, not even Ki's *shuriken,* but it was time—it was the best chance they had had, the best they might ever have.

"Now," Ki said so softly that his voice hardly carried to Jessica who looked into his eyes, making sure that she had made no mistake in what she heard. Ki nodded and shifted the broom slightly. He began backing toward the hallway, his head inclining again, urging Jessica to follow.

She bolted out of her chair and all hell broke loose.

Mono hadn't been as sleepy as he had looked, nor had the Indian, Halcón, and another man to Ki's left. The Indian grabbed at Jessie as she passed his chair, caught her sleeve, and yanked her back. Jessie went for his eyes with stiffened fingers, but Halcón was able to turn his head away. He fell back over his chair and regained his balance, still gripping Jessica's sleeve tightly.

He laughed out loud at her temerity. He hadn't counted on any trouble from the peon who was sweeping up the cantina. But he got plenty of it.

Ki was a man of the martial arts and he had a weapon in his hand. The broom.

Once Ki had spent many, many hours working with a master of the art of fighting with a staff. The broom was close enough to a weapon. Ki turned on one heel and brought the handle of the broom up into Halcón's midsection, driving the air painfully from his diaphragm. The bandit *oof*ed and plopped back into his chair, losing his hold on Jessie's arm.

To Ki's left, a bandit drew his revolver and aimed it with liquor-fogged eyes. Ki's broom seemed simply to swat the gun away. The Mexican howled with pain and clutched at his broken wrist.

Jessie was darting toward the corridor as Ki spun again, unleashed a stunning backward kick that landed on Mono's heart, and followed with the handle of the broom. He struck the bandit leader above the eye and rocked him back on his heels.

A bullet flew across the room, punching a hole through a barrel near Sanchez's head, and Ki chose the better part of valor, making his own dash toward the corridor and hurling himself the last few feet as three or four more bullets ripped at the adobe walls, spattering Ki with plaster.

Jessie was at the end of the corridor, poised at the door opening to the alley. As Ki watched, the door popped open and Arturo, clawing at his sleep-encrusted eyes, entered the corridor.

Ki had been expecting that and he never stopped his running motion. With a cry of combat rising to his lips, Ki executed a flying kick that sent Arturo reeling back into the alley, clutching his throat. Ki took Jessie's hand, leaped over the thrashing bandit's body, and raced up the alley.

Mono and his men were tight on their heels. A fusillade of bullets traced their way through the alley, slamming into walls, penetrating barrels and piles of splintered lumber, and ricocheting crazily into the dry, bright day.

"There!" Ki said, and Jessie threw herself into the

mouth of a connecting alley, Ki following right behind.

"Which way now?" she asked breathlessly.

Ki answered, "The church. Maria said it was safe there. The church, Jessica, hurry!"

There wasn't much time for discussion, so Jessie went along with the idea. From behind them, they could hear much cursing, the rush of boots and Mono shouting a hysterical command.

They crossed the plaza without being seen, entered yet another alley, and circled toward the mission church. The heavy gates were shut and presumably barred. Jessie was breathing heavily; Ki's heart raced in his chest. Any second now, any second Mono and his gang would appear at the head of the street and that would be that. The guns would open up and what was left of their corpses would be on the way to Don Alejandro.

Ki reached the gate first and pounded on the heavy oak planks with the heel of his hand, but there was no response from within. None at all.

"Ki!" It was Jessica who saw a gate open, saw a cassocked figure waving an urgent hand. They ran to the small gate and slipped through just in time. Mono was rounding the corner farther up the street, red-faced, hatless, shouting at his men, and threatening them with death and worse if they didn't find the *gringa* and the Chinaman.

Jessie and Ki could hear his ringing curses, his violent threats, as they followed the friar with the shaved head up a thickly overgrown garden path to a side entrance to the great mission church.

Inside it was dark, cool, still.

"This way," the friar said and he led them to a wall panel that sprung open magically at his touch. A flight of adobe stairs led downward into a vast, dark chamber.

"In other times," the friar said, "we of our order hid from the king's emissaries of violence."

Mono's emissaries of violence couldn't have been far

behind. Jessica Starbuck and Ki didn't need a second invitation to follow the friar into the hidden chamber.

At the bottom of the stairs, there was a narrow, high-ceilinged alcove with a heavy Spanish table and six chairs. Maria sat in one of these.

She rose and came to Ki, hugged him, and drew a curious glance from Jessica Starbuck.

The priest had hung the lantern on the wall, and he turned now, folding his hands.

"I am Brother Joseph, rector of the *Misión de San Ignacio*. You are welcome to stay here for as long as you must."

Jessica replied, "Thank you. Will there be trouble with Mono over this?"

"There is always trouble," he said. "He will come and search the church perhaps, but he will not find you here."

They heard a thump on the ceiling, then two more thumps. Brother Joseph said, "We have visitors. Just speak quietly, if you will."

"I never thought you'd make it, Ki," Maria said. "You had me frightened."

Ki, who was untying the ropes Jessie still wore on her wrists, answered, "I frightened myself just a little. I wouldn't want to try it again."

"What will you do now?" the friar asked. "Wait until dark and slip away? Or is it safer to wait a few days?"

"We'll make that decision later," Jessica said. "If there is any way to get a couple of horses, I can pay you for them. We'll need horses on our ride south."

"South?" Maria Sanchez shook her head, not understanding. "But your home is north."

"Yes, it is, but the house of Don Alejandro is to the south."

"Don Alejandro? The slaver?"

"That's right. This is all his doing, and if you think," Jessie said heatedly, "that he's going to get away with this, you're mistaken. Isn't that so, Ki?"

"It's something we should talk about, Jessica."

"He's cartel, Ki. He's cartel and he's a slaver and he's got a bounty out on us."

Brother Joseph looked from one to the other, not catching all of this. "The cartel?"

"We'll explain when there's time. Let's just say that Don Alejandro is a criminal and an enemy of ours."

"But what could you possibly do?" the friar asked. "With a powerful man like this, how can you hope to win?"

"We'll see," Jessie said. "Ki and I have handled situations like this before."

Ki looked doubtful. Jessica could be headstrong at times and Don Alejandro appeared to be a formidable foe. Maria spoke up. "You will handle him as you handled Mono, perhaps?"

Jessica smiled, but there wasn't a great deal of humor in it. They heard another thump, but this one wasn't a signal. Something crashed to the floor and seemed to splinter.

"The rectory—they're tearing it apart," Brother Joseph said. He crossed himself and added, "I'm going up. They'll wonder where I am."

"Is it safe?" Maria asked.

"If you mean will they hurt me—no. If you are asking if they will realize where I have come from, I don't think so. I have another way to go . . . a way which, if you will excuse me, for our own safety no one not in my order must know about. If you would perhaps turn your backs."

Ki glanced at Jessie, shrugged, and turned away. They heard a small sound, rasping and hollow, and then the friar was gone. They turned to face the empty chamber.

"Very useful," Ki murmured. He had seen such things many times in Oriental temples. The monks there had also had cause to conceal themselves at times. And from time to time to conceal a wandering fugitive warrior.

"You can't let this woman talk you into fighting Don Alejandro," Maria said, but she drew no response from Ki. She took his arms and turned him to face her. "It is death to do battle with him. He has more soldiers than Mono, although it is said that Mono can call a hundred men to him anytime he wishes. Don Alejandro has a virtual army and he keeps them around him."

"What will be will be," Ki said, an answer Maria found flippant and distinctly unsatisfying.

"If I have to," Jessica Starbuck said, "I can find some pretty good fighting men of my own. Don Alejandro can't hide behind his army."

"And I thought I was a strong-willed woman," Maria Sanchez said with an exasperated sigh. "For now, however, Don Alejandro does not matter, does he? We are trapped by a very small and very violent army. Mono is up there and he will find us. It is a dream even to think we can slip away into the darkness. He will find us in time. He will find us and kill us—unless we elect to remain here, to live like moles the rest of our lives."

Maria sounded just a little hysterical. That was understandable; the past day and night had been enough to strain anyone's nerves.

Unfortunately, she was right about the main point. They were trapped and it was unlikely they were going to slip out and cross the desert without being spotted by Mono. Since Ki had no intention whatever of living like a mole the rest of his life, there was only one option left—a frightening option.

They were going to have to take the war to Mono and finish the bandit gang once and for all.

Chapter 9

It was dark outside by the time the friar finally returned to Jessica, Maria, and Ki. He simply inclined his head and they followed him up the stairs to the church proper.

It lay in ruins. The pews had been tipped over, the altar cloths and draperies scattered, a great wooden cross torn down.

"Savages," the friar said very softly but with an emotion that bordered on outright anger. "This is the kind of man Mono is. Is he a man?"

"I'm sorry," Jessica said. "I'll pay for this damage."

"Why should you pay?" he asked in surprise. "Is it your doing?"

"In a way. Besides, I've got the money to do it."

The friar shrugged as if to say, whatever pleases you. He stopped, picked up a small item of cloth, and kissed it, crossing himself.

"We can eat in the rectory," Brother Joseph said. "The gates are closed outside and we have watchers in the bell tower. Excuse the appearance of my chambers."

Mono had done a job on the friar's apartment as well. Nevertheless, the table had been set with simple food and they sat to eat, the friar saying a brief grace.

The meal was short, silent, flavorful. A young man in white served, bowing to Brother Joseph each time he neared the table. There was tea after dinner, and during that Ki and Jessica told the friar and a fascinated Maria about the cartel and Don Alejandro as Brecht was calling himself.

"It is nearly hard to believe," Brother Joseph said.

"That there are greedy men out there, unscrupulous men? That there are and always will be forces trying to siphon off the wealth of America?" Jessica shook her head. "It's true, all of it. It's only the scope of the cartel's operations that encourages disbelief."

"Slavery," the friar said, "I thought we had done away with that. Is it so profitable?"

"If it wasn't," Ki pointed out, "it wouldn't have flourished for so long in every nation in the world. A lifetime of labor from a man or woman without the expense of wages—yes, it's worth it; yes, it continues in parts of Mexico. Don Alejandro is behind a large part of it, which is to say the cartel is behind it. Perhaps this, more than an urge for vengeance, is behind Jessica's insistence that we must crush this man."

The friar looked to Jessica who might have added more if the door behind her hadn't suddenly opened. A small, bedraggled Mexican, sombrero in hand, rushed in.

"What is it, Domingo?" the friar asked.

The little man was breathless. "The town—Mono is destroying it. Burning it. Breaking it up."

The friar's heavy chair screeched across the tile floor as he hurriedly rose. He walked quickly toward the outer door, Jessie and Ki following in his tracks.

Outside, against the night sky, they could see the red glow of fire, the accompanying smoke. The friar said something under his breath that didn't sound particularly holy. They climbed to a parapet that ran around the bell tower and stood looking down on the pueblo of San Ignacio.

There were three different fires, one of them raging out of control in the direction of Fernando's house. Two or three men rode their horses down a street, guns firing. Someone screamed. The cantina was ablaze with light as was the general store, apparently broken into and now being ransacked.

"Animals," the friar said. "Animals!"

"What started this?" Ki asked Domingo.

"What? You, *señor*. You and the lady. Mono wants you and he says the town will be destroyed if you are not given up."

"Domingo . . ." the friar began to warn the man.

"Don't worry. I will tell no one where they are. But after a while, will Mono not guess?"

"We'll go, Ki," Jessica said abruptly.

"Yes."

The friar was the one to object. "Go where? How? Look down there near the gates. One of the *bandidos* in the shadows. I have no horses for you now, and to try obtaining them would certainly let Mono know where you are."

"And if we don't go, they're going to destroy the town," Jessie said.

"And after you are gone," the friar commented, "will Mono know that you are gone? Will he cease his persecution of San Ignacio? I think not. He will destroy us for having let you go. There is no option but for you to stay hidden."

"Or to turn them over," Domingo said. His voice was far from harsh; there was only a sadness and a little fear perhaps in his voice. "Turn them over to Mono."

"To be killed!" The friar asked, "To have their heads cut off? Even then, Domingo, will Mono stop this warfare against our people? He is in a savage temper. San

Ignacio would not be the first town he obliterated."

Ki said, "Then we have only my option."

"What option is that?" the friar asked.

"Fighting." Ki turned his dark, firelit eyes to the friar. "Fighting Mono, finishing him before he can finish the town—killing innocent people, raping, looting."

"And this you think you can do alone?" Brother Joseph asked incredulously.

"Alone?" Ki looked to the fire. "No, I do not think we can do it alone. We need allies, weapons . . ."

"Will I do?" the voice from behind them asked. Turning, Jessica and Ki saw Diego Cardero, smiling as usual and smoking a thin cigar as usual. In his hand was a small chamois sack. "Will these help?"

He tossed the sack to Ki who caught it and opened it with curiosity, with suspicion. Inside were his *shuriken,* his deadly throwing stars.

"Where did you get these?" Ki demanded.

"From Carlos." Cardero leaned against the wall behind him, blowing blue smoke skyward.

Ki put the throwing stars away as Jessica stood staring at Diego Cardero who was still tilted lazily against the wall. Where had he come from? How had he gotten in and why?

"Now you have weapons," Diego said, "such as they are—I can't understand what you do with those things myself. And you need allies. Allow me to offer my services."

"The services of a bandit?" Jessica said.

"Yes, the services of a bandit," Diego said. "Perhaps a bandit is what you need to combat a bandit."

"Perhaps." Jessie was suspicious. Still, at some deeper, indefinable depth, she trusted Diego Cardero.

"May we ask," Brother Joseph said, "why it is you wish to help us at all, Diego Cardero? You are Cardero, are you not?"

Diego bowed from the neck—a small, nearly mocking gesture. "I am he. As to why, it is simple. Your enemies are mine."

"You rode with Mono!"

Diego shrugged and flipped his cigar away into the darkness where it fell with a shower of sparks.

"I rode with him because he was a key to something I wanted."

"To what?" Ki asked.

"To Don Alejandro. You see, Jessica, that was why I could not release you—I wanted to be there when Mono delivered you to Don Alejandro. I wanted to have a way into his confidence, a way past his gates."

"And then what?" she asked.

"And then," Cardero said, "I would have killed him."

"Why?"

Diego told them. "Do you know what I am? A Spaniard, no? This is not exactly true. My father was a Spanish land surveyor, my mother a Papago Indian. I had nothing as an Indian, so I decided to make my fortune with my weapons. I became a bandit. I have robbed banks and wealthy men's haciendas. I have done many things, Jessica Starbuck, but I have never killed wantonly, never raped, never destroyed people's homes or their means of survival. I have not been good, but I am not a man such as Mono." Mentioning the name caused Diego's face to harden, to set into rigid planes.

"But you rode with Mono."

"To get to Don Alejandro. Mono is his tool. Mono has entrance to the great house. I meant to go with him. I waited for the time when we would ride to the hacienda of Don Alejandro. Waited to kill this man."

There was something terrible and cold in Diego's voice. The friar shuddered a little.

"What did he do to you?" Ki asked. "What is it that makes you want to kill Don Alejandro?"

"Simply this, my mother was an Indian, as I have told you. Frail, gentle, happy. Her life was hard and she would not allow me to make it easier for her, not with stolen money. She was a Christian and a woman of honor. She grew her corn, gathered roots and berries, and lived quietly—until the slavers came.

"The slavers came and the people of her tribe resisted—not that it did them any good against the guns of Don Alejandro's army, but they resisted. They were beaten, of course, and the young, the strong, the men were put in chains."

Diego Cardero lit another cigar and the orange-yellow light of the match revealed a taut mask.

"My mother was not young or strong. She was taken with the other old ones, the very young, the crippled—and they were slaughtered so that they could not tell the authorities what had happened and who had taken the slaves away."

Cardero said no more. He didn't have to. Jessica tried to imagine how it was—the innocents taken out and killed, the screams and crying. A small hiss escaped involuntarily from her lips.

"This is the work of your cartel?" Brother Joseph asked.

"Yes," Jessie said. "Don Alejandro is a part of the cartel. This is how they work. Ruthless and grasping."

"I understand now," the friar said, "understand why you, too, must try to go south and destroy this Don Alejandro. And, God save my soul, I can find no fault with you for wanting to end his dirty life."

The friar then turned and walked away. The fire from San Ignacio still burned and it backlighted his cowled figure.

"Am I to be allowed to fight with you?" Diego asked.

"How can we refuse? But how are you going to gain entrance to Don Alejandro's house now?" Jessie asked.

"Some other way. There will be a way, though not as simple."

Perhaps, Ki thought, by delivering our heads himself

after this is over. Ki glanced at Jessica, but no such doubts seemed to cloud her eyes.

You trust too easily, Jessica, Ki thought. She was a woman who made decisions with her heart at times and a surprising amount of the time her heart was right in its judgments. Ki only hoped she was right this time about the bandit, Diego Cardero.

The three of them found the friar in the rectory. He told them what he had done.

"Cardero is to be one ally, but I doubt he is enough. I have asked the alcalde and several men from San Ignacio to come to the church."

"Will they fight?" Ki asked.

"Quién sabe?" He shrugged and looked from Jessica to Ki and back. "Nor will I ask them. I have invited them here so that you may speak to them, so that you may ask them to fight beside you."

There was a drawback to this plan, Ki thought. More of the townspeople would know where Ki and Jessica were hiding, and perhaps it would make more sense to the alcalde and his delegation simply to turn them over to Mono rather than to try to fight the bandit leader.

Their town was burning; their people were being hurt. They might go to any length to end the savagery of Mono.

There was no other choice, however; they would speak to the people of San Ignacio and tell them how it must be, ask them to help drive Mono away or kill him.

Ki could only hope they would listen. If they didn't, they could expect another visitor—Mono would return and this time he wouldn't be satisfied until he had the heads of Jessica Starbuck and Ki in his saddle bags.

Chapter 10

The alcalde of the town of San Ignacio was named Rivera. He was squat, heavy, balding, but there was something in his eyes that said he had once been a fighter. Ki saw that and approved.

They were introduced to Rivera and the other three important men of the delegation, and then they sat around the friar's table. Fire from the town cast bright reflections on the window of the rectory. Now and then they heard gunfire from San Ignacio as Mono continued to assault the little border town.

Rivera spoke, "So you two are the cause of this destruction."

"Mono is the cause of it," Jessie answered. "We aren't the ones responsible for what's going on out there; it's the bandits, and perhaps the people of the town who have allowed Mono to have his way in the past." She spoke sharply, her eyes glinting, and Rivera, running his tongue across his upper teeth, nodded with apparent admiration. He looked more closely at the blond *gringa* now, seeing her differently.

She was a woman with a remarkable body, breasts straining against the fabric of the white blouse she wore, her face lovely and appealing. But Rivera had expected little from the woman. The man was a different story; the Oriental looked like a warrior. The alcalde had expected the man to do the talking, but there was fire in the woman as well, fire and intelligence.

"Mono would not be here if not for you," a second man, one called Contreras, said. "He would have come, drunk his liquor, watered his horses, and ridden on."

"After stealing, raping, killing."

"A few incidents always occur," Contreras said, accepting the state of affairs with amazing readiness.

Another man, Arano, said, "We are at the mercy of these men. What are we to do? We have no army garrison; not more than half a dozen men in the town have weapons. Mono sometimes comes with fifty men. We have learned not to struggle."

"Maybe it's time to learn to struggle," Jessica said. "These bandits come and have their way. Then they leave and you're all relieved. But they'll be back, again and again. I saw a man killed last night while trying to protect his wife. Perhaps next time it will be your wife, and it will be you who is killed—if you had enough nerve to walk up to Mono and try stopping things, that is."

Arano winced under that stinging remark. "If we do nothing, perhaps we will pay a price," Rivera said, "but if we do something, we know what will happen. All of us will be ruined; many of us will be dead."

"What do you think's happening out there right now!" Jessie snapped.

"Because he wants you," Rivera responded with a slight smile, "because he wants you and your friend."

"Because," Jessica Starbuck, her voice barely under control, said, "he is a mad dog and a murderer."

"What would you have us do?" the alcalde asked. San Igancio's mayor spread his hands. "I have no weapons. If I did, how would someone like me fight Mono and his bandits. They would kill me in a moment. You speak of fighting for our homes, businesses and families—what good does it do me to have a home if I am dead? What good am I to do for my family if Mono kills me and they bury me?"

"At least," Diego Cardero put in, "you would die like a man instead of hiding like a cowering dog."

Rivera didn't like that a bit. He knew Cardero as well, knew him as a bandit. "Your way of life has been the gun, Cardero. It is easy for you to speak. Besides, what are you after here? What profit is there for you in asking us to fight Mono?"

"No profit but justice."

"Justice! You don't know the meaning of that word. Caballero, you are an outlaw as bad as any of these others. I don't know what you want here, but it makes a man think to have one such as you come to us."

"Believe what you want," Cardero said. "I'm just telling you this—Mono won't stop until he is killed."

Contreras said, "Or until he has these two back."

The friar was glowering. "I have given these two sanctuary, Señor Contreras. Perhaps that means nothing to Mono. It should mean something to you."

"Yes, and the lives of my wife and children mean something as well!" Contreras wagged his head. "I am sorry, but to ask us to fight—it is something I am unwilling to do, unwilling to ask others to do."

Maria Sanchez had stood quietly in the shadows of the rectory. Now for the first time she came forward and made her presence known. "These are the men of San Ignacio? These are our respected leaders? Cowards! Fight now or watch the town burn."

Rivera's mouth was set. The eyes were no longer amused. Perhaps American women talked like that, but it was wrong for this daughter of San Ignacio to speak up.

"Go back to your father," Rivera said to her. "Go back and clean up his house. Comfort your mother."

Maria made an exasperated sound and turned away.

Chairs scraped against the floor as the three important men from San Ignacio rose. The meeting was over.

"You have given us no answer," Brother Joseph said.

"What answer can we give? I have said we are not warriors—we are not. Fighting Mono will only cause more trouble."

"You must consider this further," the friar said as he walked with the townsmen to the heavy door. "Something must be done."

"There is nothing to be done."

"Please," the friar said, taking Rivera's arm, "consider it. Consider fighting this evil, this Mono."

Simply to free his arm and get out the door, Rivera said, "We will consider it further. Yes, yes." And then they were gone, the door closing behind them. Those remaining were silent for a long while. Maria, her back still to them all, was furious. Ki and Jessie looked at each other across the table. Cardero kept his thoughts to himself.

"I am going to pray," the friar said. No one responded and he walked away silently, arms folded.

"Maybe that will do some good," Cardero muttered a bit skeptically. "These people . . . what are they thinking? When has it done any good to back away from evil and let it have its way?"

Maria commented acidly, "Now we have morality spilling from the lips of a bandit."

Cardero didn't respond to that. He stood and walked to the window to watch the fire.

"There are only ten of them, Ki."

Ki looked up with surprise. "Yes, just ten bandits."

"Do you think we could do it?" Diego mused.

"Perhaps—if everything went right. How often does everything go right?"

"Ten men," Cardero repeated, "and an entire town cowed by them."

"They'll tell Mono," Maria said. "Cowards—they'll

tell Mono where Jessica and Ki are."

"Perhaps we underestimate them," Ki argued.

"Didn't you see the fear on their faces? I did. They had already made up their minds."

"Perhaps, perhaps," Ki said. And if that were the case, Ki and Cardero would have to try taking on Mono alone. The odds for success there weren't very high.

Ki rose and stretched. "We had better rest. Whatever happens, we will need it. Where do we sleep, Maria?"

"There are sleeping chambers in the hidden basement. I will show you."

Jessica was more tired than she realized. Sleeping on the ground or in a chair with her hands and sometimes her feet bound couldn't be called restful. When Maria guided her to a small, monkish room beneath the church, it was enough to discover that the chamber had a bed with a clean blanket on it.

She nodded her thanks to Maria and began undressing even before the door had closed. Distantly she could hear shots and occasional yells. She tried to put that out of her mind. She rinsed off in the basin that had been provided, stretched out naked on the bed, and left the candle to burn itself out.

Despite the tension, she fell off to sleep easily, sleeping deeply until a dream came. In the dream a naked man entered her chamber, quietly closed the door, and stood over Jessie with his manhood standing proud, needful, until she sat up and cupped it in her hands and kissed it as his hands rested on her head.

In the dream, the man who looked for all the world like Diego Cardero, lay beside her, stroking her breasts and thighs, letting his fingers dip inside of her, touching her sweet warmth.

Then, in the dream, Jessie straddled the man, her thighs against his chest and shoulders. She sat there, her head thrown back as Cardero, or the dream man, tasted her.

When she could stand no more of that, Jessica Starbuck slid slowly down onto his ready shaft. Without using her hands, she eased onto him, feeling the pressure of his erection against the walls of her womb, feeling the steady pulsing there, the nudging of his body against hers, the clench of his hands on her buttocks.

In the dream he began to arch his back and lift himself against her as she nearly slept against his chest. He worked deftly against her, inside her, his swelling and thrusting becoming a crazy, urgent pounding that flooded Jessica with pleasure.

She rode him long, this dream man, until she felt his hot rush of release inside her and felt her own throat constricted with emotion, her breasts ready to burst. Her body trembled and seemed to explode with pleasure.

Then the night was still again and Jessica dozed. When she awoke an hour later, there was no one there. It had only been a dream.

She arose at first light, her spirits dimming as she came fully awake. She was rested at least, rested and ready for anything to come. But what was there to do?

Uncharacteristically, Ki also looked depressed this morning. Neither of them was aware of the little tragedy taking place in the main street of San Ignacio, a tragedy that would turn everything around and carry them on toward more violent tumult.

Mono was sleeping in a wooden chair in front of the cantina. Other bandits were inside on the floor. Arturo had taken the horses to the plaza fountain to water them. The fires had gone out overnight; the adobes didn't burn that well.

Arturo was in a foul mood. He had had enough of San Ignacio. The women were all hidden. He had had too much to drink. The prisoners, worth their weight in gold, had escaped. His throat still hurt where the Chinaman had kicked him.

The horses were balky and Arturo had a throbbing tequila headache. And Mono slept. They should be riding by now—forget the woman and the Chinaman, find some bank, and open it up. But Mono stayed. Mono wanted to find the prisoners, although Arturo's own idea was that they were far away by now.

The sun was already hot, the air dusty. Arturo took the horses to the fountain and watched them drink. He ducked his own head in, wiping back his long stringy hair as he straightened.

"Damn this town; damn San Ignacio," Arturo muttered.

A small boy was behind Arturo's bay horse. He was five or six and wearing a new straw sombrero. He looked at Arturo and the bandit snarled.

"Go away, boy. Get out of here."

"Whose horses are these? Are they bandit horses?"

"I said get out of here."

"Can I look at them?" the boy asked brightly.

Arturo turned, kicked out, and caught the boy painfully on the hip. The boy went to the ground, sprawling in the dust.

"Now beat it," Arturo said. "Beat it before I shoot your ears off."

"You won't shoot me."

Arturo said, "Don't bet on it." His head throbbed. The little bastard was bothering him. Arturo had never liked children, though he suspected he had some of his own somewhere.

"No, you won't. You can't do anything to me because my father is the alcalde."

"I don't care if he's the Pope. Get your ass out of here."

The next time Arturo looked the child was gone. That didn't help his headache nor the thickly coated tongue that sat like an iron bar in his mouth. There was only one way to solve everything and that was to start drinking tequila again, which was just what Arturo meant to do as soon as the horses drank their fill.

He walked behind his own bay, put his hands to the small of his back, and stretched. From the corner of his eye, he saw a rock, but it was too late to do anything about it. The boy had a good aim and he stung Arturo's bay on the flank. The horse reared up in panic, and instantly five of the ten horses Arturo was watering took off at a run down the street.

A second rock narrowly missed Arturo himself, and in a rage the bandit swung aboard his still shying bay. Ahead of him horses raced down the street.

Ahead of him as well was the barefoot smart-ass kid. Arturo saw the dark eyes look back in fear, saw the sombrero fly from the kid's head. The kid hesitated, stopped, and tried to recover his hat.

Arturo rode over the hat, trampling it, and then he rode the boy down.

There was a brief cry and for a moment the broken body thrashed in the dust. Then he was still and Arturo spat back at the body. It would take him a hell of a long time to round up those horses, and his head was throbbing with pain.

The knock on the door of the rectory brought Ki's head up. He looked to Jessie and then to the friar. Diego, who was looking over the town plan of San Ignacio, put the map aside and rested his hand near his holstered gun.

Maria looked to Brother Joseph, who nodded, and she crossed on silent feet to the door, opening it.

The man who entered was broken. His face was drawn, his eyes blank. In his arms was the body of a child, bloody and smeared with dust.

"Brother Joseph," was all Rivera said at first.

"Madre de Dios." Brother Joseph crossed himself and went to the alcalde who stood framed in the doorway, his son in his arms. "What has happened?"

"The last rites, please," Rivera said.

"Yes, yes, of course, but what has happened, Diego?" the friar asked.

Bandidos. A *bandido* . . ." the man's voice broke. His own face was dusty, teary. "One killed him, a child."

"I'm sorry," Jessica said, "very sorry. Is there anything at all we can do?"

"Yes," the alcalde answered grimly. "Show us how to fight. Show us how to kill these child murderers."

For the rest of the morning, Rivera was with the priest and his dead son, but in the afternoon he emerged to sit down at the table with Jessica, Diego, and Ki. "What is it we can do?" Rivera asked.

"Get your people together. Maybe this evening they can arrive in small groups."

"I will say it is a mass for my son," Rivera put in. It was a good idea but perhaps a bit cold. But Rivera was done with his mourning. Now his thoughts were only on venegence.

"That will work," Ki said. "We want to talk to these men and plan our action—if they will fight now. Will they, Rivera?"

"They will fight. I will see to that," the alcalde promised.

"Tonight, then. Let's not let this go on any longer than necessary," Jessica said.

"No. To put it off is to see other children die," Rivera said. "Now I see that. If I had listened to you yesterday, perhaps my son would not be dead now."

"Maybe, but don't blame yourself. It's Mono's fault, all of it, as we said before."

"Then Mono is the one who must pay, who will pay." Rivera rose and nodded to them. He didn't offer his hand. Still dusty but now erect, he went out.

"Ki? Diego?" Brother Joseph had returned. "I heard most of that. I have something to show you. Whether it is of any help or not is for you to decide."

Ki and Diego exchanged a curious glance, rose, and followed the friar downward once more and into yet another hidden chamber beneath the church.

Taking a lantern from a hidden nook, the friar lit it and entered a small chamber whose entrance was indistinguishable from the wall surrounding it.

Inside, the lantern glowed on an odd assortment of ancient objects: armor, swords, battle axes, and, standing in a neat row along a wooden rack, a file of ancient muskets.

"These firearms were taken long ago from a band of mutinous soldiers who came to San Ignacio. The friar convinced them to turn themselves in and throw themselves on the mercy of the crown." He paused. "Unfortunately, the queen ordered them all beheaded. However, their weapons survived."

Diego had picked up one of the muskets. It was fifty years old at least and not cleaned in all that time. He checked the lock of the ancient firing mechanism by cocking and letting the flint drop. Sparks were produced. He shook his head and handed the weapon to Ki.

"If the barrels aren't rusted shut, they will fire. You have powder for these contraptions?" Ki asked.

"Cans of it, yes. Whether it is good or not, I couldn't say. I have musket balls and flints and bayonets."

Ki replaced the musket. "Let's have a look at the powder."

There were six five-pound cans of it, three of them damp and decomposed, the others apparently dry. Diego went to the rack, took one of the muzzle loaders, and primed it. When he dropped the flint this time, the powder flashed brightly. "It'll work. Some of the time," he added.

"Then these will be of some help? the friar asked.

"I think so," Ki answered. "Now," he said, "all we need is some men willing to fire them."

Chapter 11

There was a new fire burning in town. From the rampart surrounding the bell tower, Ki and Jessica watched it burn.

Below them, in small groups the men of San Ignacio, dressed in their best clothes, entered the churchyard and walked into the mission. The funeral service for the alcalde's son would be held that night. A brief mass and then a meeting behind the locked and guarded church doors. A council of war.

"What do you think, Ki?" Jessica Starbuck asked. "Will they fight?"

"If they don't, they will lose their town."

"They weren't all that concerned before. They weren't eager to fight no matter what the provocation. They don't seem to be able to see that it's in their best interests."

"Then," Ki said, "it is our job to see that they discover that. The alcalde wants to fight because he has lost a son. I only hope they each don't have to lose someone before they realize that Mono must be done away with."

The men of the town were willing to listen but reluctant to make a decision. "We aren't soldiers," one man objected. "Call for the *federales;* let them dispose of Mono."

"A week to Mexico City, a week back with soldiers—how much damage can Mono do in that time? He would be gone and San Ignacio would be nothing but a memory," Jessica responded.

"We must do this ourselves," the alcalde said. "That much is clear."

"You grieve for your son. We understand your anger, Rivera, but we are not fighting men. We have no weapons."

That was Diego's cue to enter the church with his armload of muskets. He put them down with a clatter and stood, hands on hips, over them.

"Here are your weapons. Where are the men to use them? the bandit asked.

"These rusty toys against Mono's repeating rifles!"

"They will cut us to pieces."

Ki spoke again. "Have you considered, that there are forty men in this room. Forty men! Mono has but ten *bandidos*. You are four to one. Ten men hold your town hostage. Ten men terrorize your women and children. Ten men and the entire town of San Ignacio is afraid of them!"

There was enough disgust in Ki's voice to cause heads to lower slightly in shame. Glances were exchanged uneasily. The men of San Ignacio shifted in the pews.

"Ten men," Ki repeated. "Each one of them can be killed with a single bullet. They have no chance at all against an armed town, a town willing to defend itself."

"The weapons," one man, braver than the rest asked, "will they fire?"

"They will. Diego Cardero and I spent most of the afternoon cleaning and oiling them. They will fire and they are deadly enough to kill any man, Mono included."

"If I ever had him in front of a gun . . ."

"Then put him there!" Jessica exhorted.

Diego Cardero said, "You are being offered a great opportunity—security for all time against these bandits.

What band of outlaws would descend on this town knowing that you once took up arms and defeated the mighty Mono?"

Speaking about it as if it were already a reality encouraged the townspeople. Two men in the back got to their feet.

"I've had enough of these roving bandits. Every year they raid my stores. Every year my wife and daughter have to hide in the hills. Every year we allow them to spit on us. Give me a gun. Show me how to work it. Show me Mono!"

Once the tide of opinion had shifted, it became a tumultuous demand for justice, for weapons, for Mono's blood. Things got so noisy that the friar had to caution them. "Quiet, please. We are not ready for battle, not yet armed. Too much noise will raise the bandits' suspicions."

"Let them be suspicious! Load a gun and give it to me. I know how to pull a trigger," one man responded.

It took some time to settle things down again, but finally the muskets were handed out—first to those who knew what to do with them, then to the most eager students who were put through their paces by Ki and Diego and by Jessica Starbuck who had handled a muzzle loader before.

That done, Ki went over his battle plan. "The bandits wander the streets now, but by midnight they will probably return to the cantina to sleep together as they did last night. There may be a guard posted; there may not be. Mono will expect no resistance at all. When has there been resistance?"

Jessica went on. "Sometime after midnight we expect to find the entire gang drunk or sleeping in the cantina. You men will begin to filter into the streets, some taking up positions on rooftops. With the sheer numbers on our side, we should be able to take Mono easily and quickly. Keep the shooting to a minimum. There's always the danger of shooting each other in the darkness. Any surviving bandits will face justice later."

"And they will!" the alcalde said vigorously.

Jessica and Ki's ragged army had become enthusiastic. Now, rather than encouraging them, it seemed important to keep the lid on.

"Each man will be shown his position on the town plan. Diego Cardero has a copy. Each man will be given a time to take up his post. Follow the plan!" Ki said with some force. "Don't lose your discipline. Above all, don't fire until I signal you. One early shot can ruin all of this."

"Do you still want me to take care of the horses, Ki?" Diego Cardero asked.

"Yes. They won't get far without their horses, even if they do break out of the cantina—though I don't see how they can even accomplish that, not with the sharpshooters on the roofs."

"And me, Ki," Brother Joseph asked, "what do I do?"

"What you're best at. Pray."

Everyone was shown exactly what to do and told when to do it. The Mexicans slipped homeward then, carrying muskets and powder. The new fire had died down. San Ignacio was silent. But it wouldn't be for long. There was going to be a lot of flame and thunder and it was going to sweep Mono and his outlaws straight to the gates of hell.

It was a long wait until midnight. Diego checked his own guns and oiled them. Jessica wore a .44 borrowed from Cardero. Ki had his throwing stars ready and was running over the plan again and again in his mind.

"Nothing can go wrong, can it?" the friar asked anxiously.

"Not if they do their parts right," Ki answered.

"If it does go wrong . . . if it does," the friar said, "we may have encouraged many good, simple men to march to their deaths."

"Nothing will go wrong," Ki repeated. Brother Joseph rested a hand briefly on Ki's shoulder and walked away. It seemed hours later when Diego approached Ki, fastening the drawstring on his black sombrero.

"It is time, amigo. Time now to finish these animals."

Ki had exchanged his peon costume for a friar's dark robe. It would prevent him being seen so easily in the darkness. Jessica was grim and silent as she met the men at the back gate. Ki looked to her and nodded and he started on.

Diego stepped to Jessie, drew her into his arms, and kissed her once. "Be careful, Jessica Starbuck," he said.

"Don't worry about me."

"But I do." Then he smiled his ingratiating smile and was gone, slipping off through the shadows cast by the mission wall toward the horses that were his objective.

Jessica hurried to catch up with Ki, who gave her a questioning look but said nothing. There was no time for further conversation.

Working their way toward the cantina, they saw no one—which bolstered Ki's confidence in his plan. The Mexicans on the rooftops were keeping their heads down according to instructions, and those moving on the streets were being very silent, staying out of sight.

From time to time they heard a footstep or a sigh, but these wouldn't be audible in the cantina. Once Ki spotted a man in a sombrero working his way up an alley, but he was doing it right, keeping to the shadows. No bleary-eyed *bandido* guard was going to spot the man or realize there was any danger.

Ki and Jessie were in the alley behind the cantina now. That was the place Ki had chosen for himself—if anyone were going to go inside, he was going to be the one.

"Here," he whispered to Jessica, nodding to the stack of used crates and discarded barrels thirty feet from the back entrance to the cantina.

"Think I can't handle the job?" Jessie whispered back.

"I want you to cover me from there. It does no good for both of us to be exposed."

Which was more or less true. Ki was protecting Jessica or trying to, and she knew it. Still, someone needed to be in a position to back up Ki if the outlaws decided to stream out the back door. Jessie shrugged, let her lips brush Ki's cheek, and moved silently behind the pile of refuse.

Ki went nearer the door and then squatted in the shadows, waiting.

First Cardero would have to lead the bandits' horses away or drive them off. That would be Ki's signal to activate the assault. The horses had to go. A man on horseback is a lousy target, a horse's body being an effective shield for a man who knew how to use it. This wasn't to be the first time Mono and his men had been in a fight. They would go for the horses first, not wanting to get caught afoot in a hostile crossfire.

Ki looked to the stars, filled his hands with *shuriken* from the pockets of the dark, cowled robe he wore, and waited.

Diego had worked his way nearer to the stable where the bandits' horses were being kept. Across the street and down two buildings from the cantina, the stable was dark and still.

But not empty. Someone was inside.

Cardero pressed himself against the wall of the stable, his pistol in his hand and pressed against his thigh. His thumb was on the hammer of the big single-action Colt.

Damn it all. A guard in the stable. That one would have to be taken silently. Cardero glanced at the rooftops opposite and saw a single man against the starry sky. Everyone was ready, in position. But the horses had to go.

Except it wasn't going to be easy.

Diego heard a horse shift its feet and then blow through its nostrils. A little while later he heard the squeak of saddle leather and he frowned. Someone was in there all right, but he wasn't standing watch; he was swinging into a saddle and preparing to ride out.

Did that make any sense?

Cardero hesitated. Let the man ride out if that was what he was going to do? he wondered. Or try to take him and risk alerting Mono?

There wasn't much time for a decision. The side door of the stable opened, and a man on horseback, ducking to clear the door, walked a black horse out into the side alley. Cardero's gun came up, but he lowered it again. Silence was more important than taking out one man.

He watched from the shadows as Halcón turned his horse toward the river, walking it for a quarter mile before he broke into a gallop.

And what was it Halcón was doing? Had the Indian finally had enough of Mono himself? There wasn't time to ponder Halcón's motives. Cardero was already behind his schedule. Ki would be wondering what was happening; the men on the rooftops would be growing uneasy and anxious.

Diego took a slow, deep breath, holstered his gun, and moved into the darkness of the stable, walking toward the first of the string of horses, which happened to be Mono's own sorrel.

Before he reach it, guns opened up and deadly thunder filled the streets of San Ignacio.

Chapter 12

It wasn't until later that Ki and Jessie found out what started the firefight. A Mexican on the roof opposite the cantina, already jittery, tired from the night's watch, and eager to use the musket he had been given, saw Mono.

Mono, after waking from his stupor, had gone to the door of the cantina to breathe in some night air and to clear his head before, accompanied by another bottle of tequila, he went back to sleep to dream his dreams of vengeance agains the *gringa* and her Chinaman.

The massive, bearded bandit made a stark, wide target against the doorway of the cantina, lighted as it was by a lantern from within.

The eager townsman, his hands trembling and his mouth dry shouldered the heavy, ancient weapon and fired.

The flash scorched the Mexican's face. The musket ball flew past Mono's head, smashing the glass behind the bar.

Mono was drugged with liquor and sleep, but he was a man who lived on the fringe of violence or at its vortex, so he was instinctual and quick in his response. He drew his twin Remington revolvers and unleased a barrage of bullets at the rooftop. One bullet caught not the man who had fired the shot, but another beside him who had been diving at the sniper, trying futilely to stop him. He stood up, clutched his belly, and fell awkwardly to the street below, landing on his head. The sniper, trying desperately to reload, missed his footing and also fell, but he was able to drag himself back into an alley, his broken leg digging a furrow in the dusty road.

"*Hombres,* ambush!" Mono was yelling. He saw a target to his left, wheeled, crouched, and fired with one gun. Mono was a good shot. The bullet took the legs from under the fleeing Mexican, and he went down, crippled by a slug through the hips.

A chair crashed through the front window of the cantina, scattering shards of glass across the plankwalk. In the window Arturo and Miguel, rifles ready, began to lay down a withering barrage of bullets, and Ki's snipers panicked, some throwing down their weapons and fleeing across the rooftops as the bandits' repeating Winchesters spat flame. Staccato snaps and roars filled the night with sound.

The lantern in the cantina had been smashed at the first shot, and now from the darkness the bandits fired, offering no targets but their muzzle flashes.

Mono, crouching low, moved inside and directed the fire. The Mexicans, racing frantically across the rooftops opposite the cantina, were distinct against the starry sky. They weren't clear targets, but Mono's men had fought often and fought well. They knew what their Winchesters were for.

A Mexican, leaping from one roof to the next, was caught in the middle of his jump by a spinning .44 slug, and he was dead before he reached the opposite side. He slammed into the roof, slid down, and lay still.

In the back alley, Ki groaned and looked to where Jessica crouched, covering him. Something had gone wrong. The trap had failed. Ki saw fleeing men, muskets in their hands, rushing blindly past him, and he tried to rally them.

"Stop! We still have them beaten! We have Mono outnumbered."

One man stopped; the others raced on, one throwing his musket away. The back door of the cantina popped open, and a bandit with a sombrero hanging by its draw string and his hands filled with two revolvers, appeared, looking frantically up and down the alley.

A *shuriken* from Ki's hand whipped through the air and tagged the outlaw in the throat, ripping open trachea and jugular. He was dragged back inside by an unseen friend, blood smearing his shirt. The door was barred and Ki, in frustration, flipped another throwing star at the door.

The *shuriken* imbedded itself deeply in the wood, but it could do no damage. They wouldn't be coming out that way again.

"Jessie!"

"Right here!"

Jessica Starbuck was right behind Ki, her pistol raised and cocked, but without a target.

"Around the front. Mono will try for the stables now."

And that was just what Mono was planning. Before Jessica and Ki had circled the building and reached the main street of San Ignacio, Mono, leading his men and scorching the night with a savage burst of gunfire, came out onto the plankwalk. With both pistols blazing away at the overwhelmed snipers on the rooftops, Mono led his soldiers toward the stable.

Diego Cardero was alone there, but from the doorway he opened fire. One bandit went down, crumpling into a scarcely human ball and sending dust spewing up into the night.

Mono roared. His voice was inaudible above the booming of the guns. His mouth was open in a savage cry, his head thrown back. He had seen Cardero, recognized him. Now his rage at being betrayed flooded his massive body with bloodlust. Mono's pistols exploded in his thick hands; the bullets he sent flying toward Diego ripped at the wooden stable door. One bullet tagged a horse high on the hip and the frightened, wounded animal broke free of its tether, rearing up to gallop frantically out the side door.

Cardero fired back once and then the hammer of his Colt dropped on an empty chamber. He reloaded hastily as Mono and his bandits charged on toward the stable, sending lead in all directions. Red streaks shot from the muzzles of their weapons.

Diego, alone and besieged, snapped the cylinder back in place and emptied his gun in the direction of the outlaws. He thought he tagged another man, but it was hard to be sure in the night.

Sweat streamed down Cardero's face, although the night was cool. From behind a water trough, a *bandido* winged a few shots at Diego, one coming so close that it tugged at the loose sleeve of his shirt and tunneled into the wall behind him.

"Diego!" Jessica Starbuck called out. Cardero turned. Behind him was a bandit who had somehow slipped into the stable unnoticed. The warning was unnecessary. The man was already dead, a razor-edged *shuriken* imbedded in his forehead.

Some involuntary action of the nerves caused the bandit to seem to wink at Cardero, and then with blood smearing his face, he toppled over, dead.

Jessie and Ki were beside Diego now, and they fought back furiously, driving Mono to the shelter of the buildings across the street.

The muskets on the rooftops had fallen silent now, and except for an occasional shot from the head of the street, Ki, Jessie, and Diego Cardero fought on alone. It wasn't enough. Mono couldn't get to his horses, but in a sudden unexpected move, the bandits, rushing back up the street returned to the comparative safety of the cantina where, warned and ready, they could now barricade themselves and hold off any army.

It was over. San Ignacio was abruptly still. Gunsmoke still hung in the air above the street. Not far away a bandit moaned with pain. After another minute the bandit lay still, and the night breeze off the river dissipated the smoke.

Ki straightened up and looked at the street. There was a cold anger in him, an emotion that he tried to stifle. But it remained near the surface.

Diego voiced Ki's feelings, "Bastards blew it for us. Opened up on Mono before we were ready and then panicked and took to their heels. The stupid bastards."

"They aren't soldiers," Jessica reminded them quietly. "Just men trying to protect their homes, not really up to it."

"You're right, of course," Diego said, running a hand across his hair.

"Our position isn't so bad," Jessica said thoughtfully.

"What do you mean?"

"Look at it. We've got Mono bottled up. How long can he hold out there? A couple of us can stand watch. Perhaps call another meeting. Damn it, convince the people of San Ignacio that we've won. We can starve Mono out eventually."

"The lady's right," Diego said. He reloaded his gun and holstered it. He lit a cigar, crossed his arms, and stared across the street at the cantina. "Damn all, she's right isn't she, Ki?"

"She is right. Of course, Mono will try to break loose again, but we can hold him in there. There's nothing to stop us now from getting the horses out of the stable."

"Stuck," Diego Cardero said. "The man's stuck."

Ki said, "If we get our army back."

"We—" Cardero started to say something, but sudden violence interrupted him. He saw movement. Cardero was fast on the draw and good with a gun, but he knew he was never going to turn and fire before the bandit, who had appeared in the stable behind them, could cut the three of them down with the scattergun he held in his hands.

Cardero shoved Jessica to one side, turned, and drew. The bandit with the shotgun didn't cut loose; the flame and thunder of the ten-gauge was held back.

Then as Cardero watched, the bandit pitched forward onto his face, dead. An arrow quivered in his back.

"What the hell . . .?"

Ki's eyes searched the darkness. He placed his hand on Cardero's wrist, and the bandit reluctantly holstered his gun again.

"Come out now; we know you're here and we know what you want," Ki said. Jessica could only look at Ki with puzzlement. Who was there?

After a moment her question was answered. From the darkness an Indian came forward, bow in hand. He was dressed in buckskin pants, plain shirt, soft moccasins. He wore a red headband around his head, which was fringed with unevenly trimmed, blue-black hair.

The warrior looked at Ki, at Jessica, at Cardero—a spark seemed to pass between these two—then he crouched and cut his arrow from the *bandido*'s back, replacing it in his soft deerskin quiver.

"Who is he?" Jessie asked. "What does he want?"

"The Cañon del Dios, Jessica," Ki responded. "Remember the man watching us from the bluffs? This is the man who killed Carlos when he attacked you. Who he is, I don't know, but he has been following us southward for many days. Who are you?" Ki asked the man directly. There was no answer. Ki asked him again and got the same negative response.

Cardero spoke up. "He is Papago. I will ask him." The bandit said, "You forget, it is the language of my mother's people." The bandit spoke to the Indian who was reluctant to answer at first. Finally he did reply in a brief, angry spate of words.

Cardero translated. "His name is Fly Catcher. A Papago of the Cañon del Dios. Squirrel was his cousin. Squirrel had sold out his own people to the slavers, to Mono. Fly Catcher's wife of two weeks was taken. His idea was to follow Mono to where his woman had been taken. He saw you and Ki taken prisoner. He determined to try to help you, but not at the risk of letting Mono take him as well. He was watching when Carlos attacked you at Tinajas Caliente. He killed Carlos. He would like to kill me, I think," Cardero said. "He knows I was with Mono, knows that I have Papago blood in me. He calls me a—well, there's no English word for it—a sort of bastard traitor."

"And what does he want now?" Jessica asked.

"To fight, only to fight."

Ki said, "Tell him we need warriors badly. Tell him we welcome Fly Catcher to our war. Tell him this also, Cardero, that when this battle is over Jessica Starbuck and I are going to the ranch of Don Alejandro and then his wife shall be freed."

"I will tell him," Cardero said, "that all of us are going to see Don Alejandro. You haven't forgotten my business with the slaver, have you?"

"No," Ki said with reserve, "I haven't forgotten." But was that Cardero's real purpose for wanting to go with Jessie and Ki to the ranch of Don Alejandro? Or did he still have his eyes on the bounty that had been offered?

"We'd better get back to the church, Ki," Jessica said.

"Yes. Things have to organized again and quickly. Diego, you and Fly Catcher will stay here to watch the cantina."

"As you say, Ki," Cardero said with a hint of mockery.

"Mono will be hesitant to try anything for a little while. We'll try to get reinforcements back here quickly."

Cardero simply bowed from the neck; they saying

something rapid and brief to the Papago, the Spaniard faded into the shadows once more, the silent Papago beside him.

"And what do you think now, Jessie?" Ki asked.

"Cardero?"

"Yes. Do you still trust him?"

"I want to, Ki. I want very much to trust that man."

So did Ki, but he knew that wanting something and having it become a reality weren't the same. There was something too supercilious, too bold about this Cardero. He was a reckless, admittedly criminal man. And he was good with a gun—too damned good. Ki had seen him draw and whirl as Fly Catcher put an arrow into the back of the bandit in the stable, and he knew one thing about Diego Cardero. He was a man even Ki did not wish to face in a fight to the death.

Cardero watched Jessie and Ki go. He took up a post in the hayloft, smoking his usual thin cigar. The Papago had drifted away, but Diego wasn't worried about that one. He was a solitary hunter, a warrior of the shadows. He would do his part.

Diego realized then that he had forgotten in all that had happened to tell Ki that Halcón had ridden out alone just before the battle started. He turned that over in his mind, considered going after Jessie and Ki, and then shrugged the concern away. What did it matter what Halcón was up to. What did they have to fear from a single rider?

Cardero settled in with his cigar and his guns and watched the slow, bloody night pass.

Chapter 13

Surprisingly, the mission was ablaze with light, but then the need for secrecy was gone. Mono was beaten. He was beaten, but it would still be necessary to convince the inhabitants of San Ignacio that it was so.

Jessie put it into words. "If he decided to attack again, there won't be anything standing in San Ignacio. If he comes out of that cantina, Ki, he's going to destroy everything he sees, kill any person he enounters."

She was right, Ki knew. He didn't mean to let it happen. Inside the mission a meeting of sorts was already being held in the rectory.

Rivera was holding forth and he was furious. "To throw your weapons away . . ." he was ranting as Jessica Starbuck and Ki entered the room to view the ragged, disconsolate army that had gone out not long ago so full of fervor and courage. "You, Guerrero, where is your gun? Cristobal, why did you run away from your position?"

"You know why," someone snapped. "Mono was attacking us. His men are killers. They have repeating weapons and they know how to use them. What were we to do? Stand there and be slaughtered?"

"Yes, damn you, if that's what it took!" The alcalde was wild with anger.

Ki decided it was time to take over the meeting. Maria Sanchez watched as her man walked to the front of the room—past the quiet eyes of the friar, the quizzical faces of the Mexicans.

"You did well," Ki said. It was necessary to give them some scrap of dignity to cling to, to bolster their confidence in some way. Railing at them as Rivera had been doing wasn't very helpful. "You all did well," Ki went on despite Rivera's groan, "but the job is not completed yet. Mono is beaten. We have to go now and finish the job, however."

"Beaten? How can you say he's beaten?"

"Because he is." Ki's voice was calm, reassuring.

"He drove us off, ran us out of our own town with his repeating weapons."

"He drove you off, but he lost some men. He lost his horses and with them his chance of making an escape," Ki said.

"How many men?" Rivera wanted to know.

"Three, I think. There may have been another killed. He has only five or six men left. And he's trapped in the cantina. He's got to be getting low on ammunition. He has no food for his men except the little that might be in the cantina itself. He's got nowhere to run."

"Six men," Rivera said, "and you are afraid of them!"

"It's understandable that you ran," Ki said. "All men are afraid at times. But you must understand that you have this man beaten now."

Ki looked them over. Their faces reflected every attitude from disbelief to renewed fervor. He went on, "All we have to do is return to our positions and keep him barricaded in the cantina. Some of our men were hurt tonight, some killed—this only happened because they didn't listen to orders. Standing up on the rooftops got at least one man shot. If we go about this properly and stick to instructions, no one will be hurt. Mono will have to surrender."

"He'll never let himself be hung. They'll come out shooting."

"Then," Ki said, "we shall shoot them down. There are only five or six of them. We have the advantage of position. Stay down on the rooftops! You offer no target at all that way. Are you going to let this man off the hook now? Now when you have a chance to finish it? This is for your town and your families."

"We will go back," one man said quietly.

A murmured chorus followed that: "We will go back"; "Six men, we can defeat six men"; "We'll show those bastards they can't come to San Ignacio and run things."

Rivera was satisfied, relieved. Jessica Starbuck was impatient. Only Diego and Fly Catcher were standing watch at the present time. If Mono tried to make his break soon, he was liable to succeed—at the cost of Diego Cardero's life.

"Ki," she prompted, "there's no time for more talk."

To the townspeople he said, "Now! Let us return to our positions. Stay down. You know what to do; now do it!"

Again they went out into the night. Jessica was tired. Her nostrils were still filled with the scent of smoke. The night was cool, the stars bright. Ki walked silently beside her as they worked their way toward the stable, every bit as cautious as they had been on the first excursion.

Diego wasn't there—and then he was, swinging lightly down from the loft to meet them.

"All still?" Ki asked.

"So far. Has our reluctant army returned?"

"Taking up their positions."

"We've got the son of a bitch then," Diego said confidently.

"So it appears." Ki looked around. "The horses are still here."

"I couldn't do two things at once. I'll get them out now. Jessie?"

"I'll help," she responded.

"We'll take them back along the river—in the willows somewhere." Diego hesitated. "There is one thing, Ki."

Ki lifted an eyebrow. "What?"

"Halcón. He rode out before the battle started. I meant to tell you."

"Halcón? Where in blazes would he have gone?" Jessica asked.

"He might have had enough of Mono," Ki commented.

"I thought of that." Diego Cardero was thoughtful for a moment. "Not Halcón. I don't believe it. There was something between those two. I wasn't there, but it seems to me that Mono pulled Halcón out from under the shadow of the hangman's noose at one time."

"Damn it all," Ki said very softly.

"Ki?" Jessica was surprised at the emotion in Ki's voice. "What is it?"

"Don't you remember what they told us, Jessica? I can't recall who, when, but didn't they tell us?"

"Tell us what, Ki?"

"Tell us that Mono can muster an army of a hundred *bandidos* any time he felt like it."

Jessica was stunned into silence. Diego cursed under his breath. "It's true," he said. "He can do that."

"Halcón . . ."

"Halcón could be riding for help, probably is."

"Of course, he is," Diego said.

"How far does he have to ride? How many bandits can be within a day's ride? A two-day ride?"

"Too many," Diego said. "Halcón will go there"—he lifted his eyes— "to the ranch of Don Alejandro. There are many bandits there, many."

"How long will it take?"

"I don't know." Diego shrugged. "A fast horse, a good rider . . . twenty-four hours. Maybe much less."

"This changes everything," Ki said unhappily, staring at the empty street, the square bulk of the buildings against the night sky. "Mono is barricaded in there. Eventually he would have to come out or surrender. These soldiers we have trained, Jessica, are good enough for the job we have given them. But for storming that cantina, getting Mono out before Halcón can return . . ."

"If they find out what has happened, they'll run for the hills," Diego put in. "I can't blame them. If Mono is reinforced, he'll turn San Ignacio into a pile of ashes. He's done it before. There won't be any mercy."

"And he'll find us," Jessica said with a deep sigh. "Well," she asked the men, "what do we do?"

"There's nothing much to do," Ki said, "except to fight—and to hope to God we're wrong about what Halcón is up to."

None of them clung too strongly to that hope. Halcón could have had only one reason for riding out. Mono would have his army—and soon. That meant he wouldn't consider surrender, that he wouldn't step out of the cantina until he was reinforced. That meant that Ki and Jessica had persuaded a town full of simple peasants to offer themselves for the slaughter.

"We'll take the horses," Diego said, as if that made any difference now. Still, there wasn't a lot to do but stick to the original plan.

Cardero and Jessica led the horses to the river and left them picketed there. Cardero didn't say two words the whole way there and back.

"What is it?" Jessie asked. The frogs still croaked along the dark river. The night breeze shifted the cattails. She hooked a finger in his shirt front and stood looking up at him.

"Nothing I wish to discuss," he replied.

"Secrets?"

"If you like." He smiled and kissed her smooth forehead.

Back at the stable, Ki stood watch. He glanced at Jessie and Cardero and then returned his gaze to the street.

"Nothing?" she asked.

"It's my fault, you know. I let Halcón go. I didn't want to fire a shot then, just before the battle."

"You can't blame yourself," Ki said.

Cardero didn't respond to that. Instead he said, "We've got the bear in his den but who's going to get him out?"

Jessica turned around with astonishment on her face. "You can't be thinking what I think you are."

"Why not?" Cardero asked, looking to Ki for support. "What else is there to do? Mono can't be left in the cantina. He's got to be driven out."

"What good will that do?" Jessie asked a little frantically. "If Halcón returns with more bandits . . ."

"We'll deal with that when we have to," Diego said. He rubbed his chin thoughtfully and produced another cigar from his shirt pocket. He was looking at the cantina now, looking intently.

"You have something in mind?" Ki asked.

"Smoke." Diego looked at his match and blew it out, watching the curling smoke rise into the darkness of the stable.

"You want to smoke him out? How?" Jessica asked. She didn't think much of the idea and she was letting Cardero know it.

"That," Diego Cardero admitted with a smile, "will take a little thought."

"Ki," Jessie pleaded, "don't let him try it—it's madness."

"Perhaps."

"Perhaps. But if we can get him out into the streets, finish him, and then withdraw to a more defensible position—into the hills, perhaps—we might yet save San Ignacio and its inhabitants. And," he added more coldly, "the world would be rid of the ape, Mono."

"Don't let him do it, Ki," Jessie said again, but Ki was far from sure that it was a poor idea. Dangerous, yes, but maybe it was their only alternative in this war they were apparently losing.

"I can't stop a man from doing what he feels he must," Ki answered, and Jessica Starbuck made a disgusted, hissing sound.

"You have another idea?" Diego asked. He took Jessie, turned her, and looked into her eyes. He was smiling that infuriating smile. Jessie softened a little.

"Not an idea in the world," she admitted reluctantly.

"Then let us see if this one has some merit."

The man behind them appeared like a magician's illusion. But then Fly Catcher was sometimes more of a shadow that a real man of blood and bone. He spoke quietly to Cardero in their tongue. Cardero answered, gesturing toward the cantina. The Indian nodded and pointed.

"What's up?" Ki asked.

"He thinks we can make it across the rooftops. It's a hell of a jump from the feed store to the cantina, but if we can make it, we can get to the chimney that rises from the oven in the cantina's kitchen."

"The smoke might never get out into the cantina proper," Ki pointed out.

"Might not," Cardero agreed. "We might not get to the roof. Hell, we might not get across the street, Ki, and you know it.That's no reason for not trying."

"No," Ki agreed. "It is no reason."

Cardero was a brave man and a good warrior. Still, Ki couldn't shake the feeling he had that there was something more to the mystery of Diego Cardero, despite what he had told them about his motives for wanting to get to Don Alejandro. Did he really have to join Mono to do that? Or was it for sheer profit that he had joined the bandit leader?

One fact was indisputable. Cardero was willing to lay his life on the line now to try to smoke Mono out of his den. It was a long chance, but it was a chance. Ki nodded agreement.

"What do you want us to do?"

"Let's scrounge some rags first, plenty of them. Tie them into big bundles. Then let's find some kerosene. And," he added, "one match."

Cardero grinned and even Ki had to admire the man's poise and confidence. Of Fly Catcher he had no doubts whatsoever. He was a skilled and determined man. His thoughts were focused on one objective, hurting the slavers—hurting the slavers and getting his wife back.

Rags were easy to come by—old horse blankets and discarded cloths filled a small cupboard in the back of the stable. Kerosene, used for lanterns, was found in a five-gallon can in the same cupboard.

Cardero tied the rags into bundles and soaked them with kerosene. When he was finished, he looked to Fly Catcher. The Papago didn't speak, didn't so much as nod. He simply turned and started away into the darkness.

He was a warrior going out to war just as the men in his tribe had done for thousands of years. The enemy was there, just across the street, and the time had come to destroy the enemy of the Papago people.

The time had come to kill the slavers.

★

Chapter 14

Ki, who usually shunned firearms but who was expert with them, snuggled down behind the sights of Cardero's Winchester. Only a rifle would do in this situation; Ki's *shuriken* rested in the pockets of his borrowed monk's robe. The sight on the Winchester swept across the front window of the cantina, the closed and barred door. Anyone appearing at door or window would be shot down. This was no time for mercy.

Jessica Starbuck also held a rifle. Her eyes lifted frequently to the rooftops. She had trouble concentrating on her primary task—covering the two silent men who worked their way toward the cantina roof. Bundles of rags were strapped to their lithe and agile bodies. Their minds were intent on the death of Mono and his *bandidos*.

Diego boosted Fly Catcher to the roof of the grain store, and the Indian reached down to tug Cardero up. Then the two men worked to the opposite side of the roof and paused there a minute.

"That's a hell of a jump," Jessie said to Ki as they watched.

"They'll have to get a running start," Ki answered.

Ki was right. As they watched, Fly Catcher retreated a little way and then began a mad dash toward the edge of the roof. He flew threw the air, arms windmilling, and landed with amazing softness on the roof of the cantina.

"They'll hear them," Jessie told Ki.

"They won't be able to do anything about it if they do hear them. The bandits can't shoot through the roof."

Cardero had backed up, and now he ran toward the gap between the two buildings, launching himself into space. He missed and Jessie gasped. His boot toes scraped the edge of the roof and slid back into the void beneath him. Fly Catcher grabbed his arm just in time and drew him up and onto the roof.

They could see Cardero lie still for a long minute as if he were catching his breath. He rose to a kneeling position and then stood, glancing once toward the stable.

"They'll make it," Ki said. "They've gotten to the chimney."

And Cardero and Fly Catcher were at the chimney. Jessie saw a match strike, a small, glowing point of red light against the darkness. Then there was a larger, brighter glow as the kerosene on the rag bundle Diego held caught fire and was dropped into the chimney.

Smoke billowed into the air. Bundle after bundle was forced into the chimney and then the chimney mouth itself was closed with a dry bundle of rags. What smoke there was now only had one direction to go—down into the cantina's kitchen.

"Get ready," Ki said. If things worked out properly, Mono and his bandits, choking and gasping, would burst from the cantina, guns blazing, to be met by a murderous answering barrage of bullets.

Things didn't work out properly at all. In fact, the daring project turned to disaster within minutes.

Jessica Starbuck and Ki saw the two men on the rooftop begin working their way back and then Jessie saw something that stopped her heart cold.

"Ki!" she cried out loudly. Below Diego and Fly Catcher in the alley, a man had appeared. It might have been Arturo—things moved too quickly to be sure. The *bandido's* rifle boomed as Diego Cardero leaped for the roof of the feed store across the alley and it was obvious that Cardero was hit.

Diego landed awkwardly roughly, on the rooftop, rolling to one side and clutching his chest. Fly Catcher had been ready to leap, but now he drew back as a second bullet cut the night, chipping plaster from the wall of the adobe, inches from the Papago Indian's head.

Jessie opened up with her rifle. Four spinning .44 slugs creased the darkness between the stable and the cantina, and Arturo—if that was who it was—fell back, firing his own rifle from his hip, levering through five, six, seven slugs until his repeater was empty. Bullets scored the walls of the stable around Jessie and Ki. One bullet caught an iron hinge on the door and whined off erratically into the night.

Fly Catcher leaped and Arturo could do nothing about it, he was behind a barrel, thumbing cartridges into the magazine of his weapon frantically.

Ki had begun to fire now as well, his carefully sighted shots peppering the rain barrel, which must have been full of water. There was no evidence that any of the bullets penetrated the far side of the barrel, and in another moment, Arturo, his rifle fully reloaded, aimed a deadly swarm of bullets at Jessie and Ki, who kept their heads down while Arturo made his escape.

Cardero was still down on the rooftop.

Now from the cantina windows, the bandits opened up; perhaps they believed they were under a full-scale attack. Perhaps the smoke within had maddened them. Ki hoped it was the latter, although there were no signs of smoke issuing from the broken cantina windows.

From the surrounding rooftops, the unorganized San

Ignacio militia opened up, firing into the cantina. This fire didn't do much to chase the bandits away from the windows. The entire Mexican force seemed to have fired their weapons at first and were now simultaneously and laboriously reloading.

As if a cease-fire had been called, the guns from the cantina halted also, and the street was deadly silent. Jessica's ears rang still. She looked to the rooftop opposite and saw that Cardero and Fly Catcher were gone, and in another minute the two men hobbled into the stable, Diego holding his chest and leaning heavily on Fly Catcher's shoulder.

"Didn't expect that," Diego panted. "Didn't expect that bastard to be in the alley."

"Shut up," Jessica said, "and lie down. Over there on the straw. How bad is it?"

"Haven't looked. Hurts like hell."

"Most gunshot wounds do." There wasn't much sympathy in her voice. Maybe she was still angry with Diego for having tried this foolhardy stunt.

"Smoke. Any smoke, Ki?"

"I don't see any."

"You will—have to."

Ki nodded, though he figured if he hadn't see it yet, he wasn't going to see any fire and smoke. Mono had gotten it out. He didn't say any of that to Cardero who was lying back on the straw, bleeding profusely.

Jessie tried to stem the flow of blood but wasn't having much luck at it. Fly Catcher put his bow and quiver aside, took a rawhide sack from around his neck, and got to work.

He sprinkled some sort of powder on the wound—Ki guessed it was powdered deer antler, but couldn't tell for sure. Whatever it was seemed to coagulate the blood some so that Fly Catcher could get to work with something else from his medicine sack: a steel needle and deer-gut thread.

The Indian's hands were deft and knowing. Fly Catcher had seen battle wounds before. When he finally straightened up and indicated to Jessie that he was through, the wound had been closed tightly, the blood flow slowed. The bullet that had caught Cardero had cut through his chest muscle from side to side, burning a bloody groove across Diego's body but luckily causing little permanent damage.

Cardcro wouldn't lie still. He struggled to his feet, making his way to the door where Ki still stood watching the cantina.

"No smoke." Diego chuckled a little. "What the hell—we tried. And what now, Ki? What exactly do we do now?"

Ki had no answer. The choices were to assault the cantina and lose a lot of people or wait and get caught between Mono and Halcón coming with reinforcements. There wasn't a hell of a lot of pleasure to be derived from contemplating either alternative.

"Ki?" Jessica asked, but he was silent, strangely silent, and Jessie knew that they were in deep trouble, very deep trouble indeed.

Dawn brought no change in their situation. Ki's eyes were heavy. The men on the rooftops would be haggard from a night's watching with their nerves on edge.

"We should send half of them home," Jessica said. "They won't be of any use to us if they're falling asleep up there."

Cardero said, "They won't be much use to us at home." But either way it probably didn't matter—not if Halcón brought help. Mono had to be extracted from the cantina before Halcón came. How long did they have? A day? Two?

"There must be a way," Ki said as if he had been sharing Diego's thoughts, "some way."

"If we could—" Diego's words were cut off by a shout

from a sentry atop the roof next door. Ki turned around and looked up into the brilliant morning sun.

"Now what?"

The man was waving his arm furiously and now others rose mirroring the gesture. Ki started up the side alley at a run, Jessica at his heels and Diego hobbling behind. He reached the rooftop in minutes and had time to look out toward the south where the sentry was pointing before Jessica joined him.

"What is it, Ki?" she asked, already afraid that she knew the answer.

"A body of men, many men, riding this way."

"It can't be Halcón—not so soon."

"Can't it?" Ki asked, shading his eyes against the glare of the sun. "Who else can it be?"

"Not so soon," Jessica said.

"Perhaps he met Don Alejandro riding north for some reason. Riding to find us, to see how his plan had succeeded for instance."

"Ki . . ." Jessie's mouth dropped into an unhappy frown that tightened minutes later into anger. Around them the peons stood in bewildered pairs or alone with ancient, futile weapons in their hands.

Diego, with a deal of effort and a lot of help from Fly Catcher, had just achieved the rooftop. Now the bandit stood—bare-chested, bloody, staring southward. He finally turned to Ki and Jessie and told them the news they had feared.

"Halcón—that's his horse in the lead."

The peons overheard him and there were angry shouts, fearful cries, and anger directed at Ki and Jessie.

"Six men you told us! We would have to fight six men. You told us Mono was defeated. You have cost us our town, our lives, the lives of our families!"

Ki didn't argue with them. How could he when apparently they were right?

"What now?" Jessica asked practically.

"The mission." Ki looked to the structure with its imposing bell tower now framed in brilliant sunlight. "It's the only place near enough, the only place we have a chance."

If they had a chance at all. The Mexicans were in near panic. One who had been sitting stood up and was shot down by bullets from the cantina.

"We're all going to be slaughtered!" one of the townsmen yelled. He started to throw his weapon down, but Diego Cardero shifted his hands slightly so that they were near his holstered gun.

"Throw that musket away and I'll shoot you."

Jessica didn't approve of the method, but it worked. She was crouched now, glancing southward where the long line of horsemen was approaching quickly.

"Ki!" she called, nodding at the Mexicans in the streets below. They were running for their homes and Ki growled under his breath.

Ki told those around him; "Get your families. Quickly. Don't stop for blankets, for food, for anything! Get to the mission—and bring your weapons!"

"We haven't got a chance," someone wailed. Ki didn't respond to that. How could he when he felt much the same himself?

"Any ideas?" Diego asked dryly. He was unsteady on his feet, the loss of blood beginning to tell on him.

"None at all. Jessie, to the mission. Fast."

They reached the street again as the guns in the cantina opened up once more. The citizens of San Ignacio had gotten careless in their blind panic. Some of them had exposed themselves blatantly. A peon lay crumpled in the center of the main street.

With the guns still roaring, Jessie, Ki, Diego, and Fly Catcher made their way back toward the mission. People were streaming toward its shelter. Women with children in arms, old men, dogs.

To the south of town, the first shots from the newly

arrived force sounded. Jessie looked at Ki, but there was nothing he could say—now they would be the besieged, Mono and his army the besieging force.

A woman slipped and fell. Ki snatched her to her feet with one arm and ran on. A bullet from somewhere whipped past his head and slammed into the walls of the old mission.

Brother Joseph was inside, waving his arm furiously. "Hurry, hurry!" he called, though there wasn't anyway they could have gone any faster. It was a headlong dash toward the supposed safety of the walled mission.

The friar asked Ki what had happened and was answered with a few brief, words.

Diego, still hobbling and helped by Fly Catcher, entered the massive gate. He was surrounded by the crush of peasants, wailing women, pale men, and frightened children.

"Get them organized," Ki said. "Up there." He looked to the wide, solid mission walls. "Everyone with a muzzle loader get on the walls. On this side—keep the retreat covered."

"You—" Jessie started to say.

"I'm going up there." Ki nodded toward the bell tower. "With a repeater I can do a job on them if they try rushing us."

"I'm going, too," Jessica said. Ki didn't take the time to argue with her.

Together they went into the church, the friar in front of them and leading them hastily to the stairwell leading up to the bell tower. They passed Maria who looked confused, angry, but not frightened. She was holding one of the muzzle loaders.

"Ki," she asked, "what can I do?"

"Stay low."

"No! I'm fighting."

"Then report to Diego. At the gate."

Maria turned away, halted, kissed Ki, and scurried on, lifting her skirts.

Jessica and the friar were already at the stairwell, Jessie peering up a long, steep, and dangerous flight of wooden steps.

"Please be careful," the friar said with all seriousness.

"Yes," Ki answered, "we will try to be."

Then, with Jessie leading the way, they climbed the four flights of stairs, past the ancient bronze bells—six of them in different sizes and used for tolling the births and marriages of the people of San Ignacio.

And for tolling their deaths.

They emerged on a small deck thirty feet square and just below the curved, uppermost bell house. Below, they could see everything that was happening, spread out in a panorama like a painting of a famous battle.

Mono had come out of the cantina and was leading his men toward the church. Southward the line of attacking raiders had nearly reached the town, chasing people before them.

The citizens of San Ignacio were still streaming toward the mission. Below, Diego had his soldiers prone along the wide wall of the mission. Puffs of smoke began to appear, rising from the muzzle of their guns. Answering puffs of smoke rose from the guns of Mono and his men, from the repeaters of the raiders. Then a sound reached Ki's ears, the distant, somehow harmless sounding reports of guns, like Fourth of July fireworks in the far distance.

A bullet from across the flats rang off the bell behind Jessie and Ki, and it rang clearly. The illusion of harmlessness fell away. The guns were coming nearer, bringing death with them.

The battle of San Ignacio had begun.

★

Chapter 15

The first wild charge the *bandidos* made was a vast mistake. Perhaps they believed the peons had no weapons or that they could simply overwhelm them with numbers and superior arms. But they were fighting from horseback and the people of San Ignacio were behind heavy adobe walls. The outlaws spent a lot of ammunition, but as Ki and Jessie found out later they actually hit only one man and that was by a ricochet. Firing from the backs of their running horses, the *bandidos* were lucky if they hit the mission walls while the peons, even considering the unreliability of their weapons and the slowness of reloading them, managed to score numbers of hits.

From the bell tower it was like shooting ducks on a pond for Jessica and Ki, armed with borrowed repeating Winchesters.

Ki put a bullet through the chest of a leading rider, and the bandit was yanked from the saddle as if jerked back by an invisible wire. Below, Diego, firing rapidly without removing his repeater from his shoulder, was able to score three hits in seven shots, taking down two horses and removing the top of the head of another bandit. An arrow from Fly Catcher's bow caught a charging *bandido* in the throat, passing completely through. He rode all the way to the gate of the mission before he fell dead.

Jessica had a shot at Mono himself, missed as the bandit leader inexplicably stumbled and went to the ground, switched her sights to a pair of riders who were trying to flank the mission from the south, and took both of them down to stay.

The *bandidos* retreated rapidly, another man falling from his horse as a musket ball bored into his spine.

Then it was still, amazingly still. The silence lasted for a long minute, and then the Mexicans along the wall set up a racket, rising to cheer, to throw their sombreros into the air, to wave triumphant muskets.

"Poor dumb bastards," Ki muttered. "It hasn't even begun yet."

And the next time it would be completely different. The first wild charge of the *bandidos* had been the result of exuberance and of badly underestimating the enemy. With their dead comrades littering the ground, that mistake wouldn't be made again.

They would come stealthily, perhaps after dark, led by Mono, and whatever they did would be carefully planned. A dozen obsolete muskets wouldn't hold back a planned assault.

"Better get them organized, Ki," Jessica said. Around her feet spent brass cartridges littered the parapet. "I'll keep watch from up here."

"Yes," Ki replied flatly, "I'd better see what can be done—if anything."

Diego, his face gray, smudged with powder smoke, met Ki below. On the walls the peons were still celebrating. Neither man commented on that folly.

"Any ideas?" Diego Cardero asked.

"Not many. Make preparations for when they breach the wall. And they will do that—given time. Barricade the doors of the church itself; give everyone instructions to fall back to the parapet up there."

"It's not enough, Ki. They have us."

"Yes." Ki didn't need to have that pointed out to him. "They have us."

There wasn't much hope of *federales* arriving at the mission in the nick of time. There wasn't much hope that a band of unorganized, poorly equipped civilian soldiers could hold off these well-equipped bandits who made war for a living.

"We'll do what we can. After that . . ." Ki shrugged.

Inside the church they met with the friar, who was anxious but determined. He walked along with them as they examined the layout of the church.

"The women and children," Brother Joseph said, "can be hidden in the basements. No one will find them there. It has been a sanctuary for two hundred years."

"All right," Ki said, "we'll get them down there as soon as possible with all the food and blankets you can scrounge up."

No one mentioned the obvious—it wouldn't do the women and children much good to be safe in the church's basements if the *bandidos* overran the church. They wouldn't be able to come up again, wouldn't be able to stay below forever.

"We just don't have enough weapons," Diego said. "If they come to the walls after dark and use any sort of judgment, they'll get over."

"We can't do a thing about it," Ki said. "There's just nothing to use."

"Olive oil," the friar said obliquely and both Diego and Ki stopped to look at the friar. Had his mind snapped?

"What did you say?" Ki asked.

"Olive oil."

"What are you talking about?" Diego asked impatiently.

"I have, if you may believe it," he told them, "made a considerable study of medieval warfare. In those time,

I believe, a weapon much in use was boiling oil rained from the walls of the besieged castle by its defenders. I have a considerable store of olive oil."

"Crazy," Diego said, dismissing the suggestion.

"I'm not so sure," Ki responded. "How much olive oil have you exactly?"

The friar waved a hand. "Hundreds of gallons. Some of it going rancid. Once the grove behind the mission was our hope for solvency. Unfortunately, there was no way to transport the olive oil to market. The grove is withering, but we have barrel upon barrel of oil in the cellars."

"Iron pots?" Ki asked. Diego was watching him as if the madness had infected Ki as well.

"In abundance," the friar said. "Hundreds of years old. They were brought from Spain at great expense, I would imagine, with the idea of giving them to the local Indians. The Indians, it turned out, preferred their own clay pots."

"Show us," Ki invited.

Diego whispered, "Ki, this will never work."

"What else have we got to try?" Ki asked. "It has worked in the past. Boiling oil is a fearful weapon when used properly."

"But can our army use it properly?"

"That is something we will discover in time," Ki answered.

The friar had moved down one of the many corridors and toward a stairway. Looking back across his shoulder, he beckoned to Ki and Diego who followed him downstairs to examine his stores.

An hour later, the Mexicans, to their confusion, were brought in to carry casks of rancid olive oil, iron pots—very rusted now—and fuel for fires to the walls of the old mission. Ki stood aside, watching. Diego muttered under his breath continually, shaking his head in wonder.

It was Maria who made the next suggestion. "Fire,"

was all she said at first, and Ki turned to look at his dark-eyed woman.

"What is it, Maria?" he asked. Her mind was turning over a problem and an apparent solution.

"Set the town on fire," she said.

"That's no good," Diego said.

"Why not? What is going to happen to the town anyway? It's mostly burned now. It will be a wonder if Mono doesn't finish it before he leaves. San Ignacio will be destroyed. Why not burn it ourselves? Use fire as our weapon. If they are caught in the fire, many might die. At least they wouldn't have the shelter of the buildings there."

"The people of San Ignacio would never stand for that," Diego objected.

"Then," Maria said practically, "we will not tell them."

It was bold enough to be unexpected, and there was a chance of doing considerable damage. Ki didn't like the idea of destroying a town he had been trying desperately to protect, but it beat having the people of that town killed. As Maria had pointed out, the odds were very good that Mono was going to destroy San Ignacio when he was through using it. Why not do it first?

"A dangerous scheme, amigo," Diego correctly stated. "Think of what is involved—slipping into town unseen and starting your fires without being caught. They have fifty pairs of eyes."

"Let's see if they won't have a few less by tomorrow," Ki replied. He had already made up his mind. After dark he would burn the outlaws' shelter down around their heads. "We're up against it, Diego. We've got to use any weapon that comes to mind."

"Including olive oil?" Diego asked with a tight little smile.

"Yes. I'll leave that to your charge. Concentrate on the gates, I think. Any other ideas?"

"Short of sticks and stones and prayer? No."

"Then we'll go ahead with this. See that half of your men are rested, will you? But put everyone on the walls after midnight. That's when they will come, I think—in the dead of the night."

"What are you going to do?"

"Sleep." Ki smiled. "I expect to have a long night."

That was just what Ki did. He went to the basement vaults and found his room. He tugged the blanket up under his chin. He was weary, nearly exhausted, but not too exhausted to feel a stirring in his groin when Maria slipped in, locked the door, and dropped her skirt.

"I want to sleep with you," she said. "Maybe this will be the last time. Maybe tomorrow . . ." She shook her head in anger and fell silent, slowly unbuttoning her blouse until her dark, ripe breasts were revealed. Then she moved to Ki's bed, her hips gently swaying, and he drew back the blanket to allow her to slip in beside him, naked and warm and wanting.

Ki slid his hand down her shoulder, across the dip of her waist, and up over her hip. Maria snuggled nearer, lifting one leg, and throwing it over Ki's thigh. She was smooth and warm and comforting against him.

"Tonight?" she asked. "Will you die tonight?"

"No," Ki said flatly.

Her hand dipped between his legs and she began to toy with his shaft, to feel it swell and lengthen.

"There has been trouble since I met you. I would like to know you when there is no trouble in your life."

Ki smiled and stroked her dark hair. And when, he wondered, has that ever been—when was there no trouble in his life? Would there ever be such a time?

He drew her mouth to his and kissed it, tasting her full lips, feeling her searching tongue press against his. Her body budged his leg and her hand began to move against his erection more urgently, to slide down its length to the base and back to the head of it where her thumb traced the sensitive head of it.

"Don't die, Ki," Maria said in a whisper.

She sat up inside his legs with a small grunt and then scooted to him, her legs going over his. Ki sat up to face her. Maria took his rod and touched it to her, letting it linger and the soft, warm entrance to her body.

Maria's arms were drapped around his neck. She scooted nearer yet, taking Ki into her. One hand dropped to feel the man where he entered her, to take him with thumb and two fingers and ease him in still farther.

She threw back her head, gasping as if she couldn't catch her breath, and Ki kissed her breasts lightly, his lips teasing her taut nipples. Maria cupped her a breast with one hand and offered it to Ki who kissed it roughly now, with tongue and teeth, tasting her woman's body, feeling her thrust against him, feeling her open to him—as she continued to sway against him, to press her heated body to his.

Ki reached behind her and clenched her ass, drawing her nearer yet, directing her rhythm, which was bringing his need to a rapidly boiling urge to complete the act.

Her lips were at his ear, his throat, his chest as she pitched her body against his. Gradually Ki lay back and Maria followed him down, her body moving against his, her hands searching for his sack, her neck arched as she gave a distant cry of joy.

Maria sagged against Ki and he began to feel the pulsing in his loins give way to necessity. He drove deeply into her and her inner muscles worked against his shaft, teasing it, adding pressure and encouragement.

"Now, Ki," she whispered into his ear, "finish it. Fill me."

Ki was a gentleman and he couldn't refuse the lady, not when she clung to him, her breath hot and moist in his ear. She begged him to reach his climax. He came urgently, his body reacting with wild, plunging strokes until he was drained and he had to hold her still and keep her body from moving against him, demanding more.

He slept and she slept beside him, keeping the night of death away for just a little while.

It was Maria who woke him hours later. She bent low and kissed his cheek. Ki's eyes opened to see the woman, dressed again, her long dark hair brushed down across her back. The candle in the corner was burning dully.

"What is it?" he asked, reaching for her leg and stroking it gently.

"It's midnight. You wanted to get up, didn't you?"

"Wanted?" Ki smiled to himself. Get up and go killing or be killed himself when there was a woman waiting, a wanting, tender woman? You lead a bitter life, Ki thought. But there were reasons he had to live that way, reasons life sometimes left a bitter taste in his mouth. There were things that had to be done and no one but Ki to do them, no others but Ki and Jessica Starbuck.

He rose, shook his head a little, and began to dress. Maria watched. Ki wore the monk's robe again. It was loose, offering much freedom, and the color was dark enough to be of some help in the night fighting. In the pockets of the robe were his silent, deadly *shuriken*. This was a night for silence and the throwing stars were the only weapon he allowed himself.

Jessica Starbuck was at the door suddenly and behind her was Diego. "Well?" Jessie asked. Her voice was just a little tense. "Time, isn't it?"

"It's time."

Diego Cardero said, "I've got—"

"You are not going," Ki said bluntly.

"The hell I'm not!"

"You're a liability, Diego. I've seen you move. That bullet has slowed you down more than you think. No, you are staying. We need a commander here anyway, someone to watch the mission forces."

"They know what to do," Diego argued.

"This is not something we can discuss, Diego. You are going to stay behind. But I do want one more man, Fly Catcher."

"Fly Catcher," Diego said with pique, "but not me."

Ki was tying a rope belt around his robe. "Fly Catcher is a silent man, a shadow, a hunter. I'm not saying he's a better warrior than you, Diego, but he's the kind of warrior I need with me tonight."

That was the end of the discussion. Diego sulked a little, but in his heart he knew that Ki was right. Ki didn't particularly like taking Jessica along, but she was determined to go, and when Jessie was determined, Ki knew he might as well argue with a brick wall.

With kerosene from the mission's stores, they started out. Fly Catcher wore the two five-gallon cans of kerosene he was carrying around his neck on a rope, leaving his hands free for his bow and arrows—another reason Ki had chosen Fly Catcher for this expedition. Fly Catcher knew how to use a silent weapon expertly.

Jessie was unarmed but for a knife and the deadliest weapon any of them carried, a box of matches.

They slipped out of the side gate and let their eyes adjust to the darkness. It wouldn't do to blunder into a wandering bandit patrol. There would be guards out somewhere—Mono wouldn't make the same mistake twice.

Ki looked toward the darkened town. From somewhere light gleamed dully. Perhaps from the cantina—nothing seemed to slow down the *bandidos'* drinking. Ki looked at Jessie and Fly Catcher and nodded, and the three of them started down a gully leading to the south side of the adobe town, Ki hoping to hell that Maria's forebodings hadn't been right, hoping that this was not his night to die.

It would be hell getting back to the mission if they were spotted. This entire foray was a long chance, but if it worked, it just might even the odds a little. It might give the people of San Ignacio a chance to live—even if it meant the death of their town.

★

Chapter 16

Jessica Starbuck could feel her pulse in her throat, at her temples, and behind her eyes. Just beyond the clump of sage where they now crouched, the gully opened up and met the back street of San Ignacio. There were three men there, watching and waiting.

Fly Catcher went to the ground and slipped from the burden of the kerosene cans he carried. He notched an arrow, pointed a finger to their right, and crept off into the darkness. Jessica had been watching him go. She could see how he vanished as he did, becoming only a silent chunk of the night.

This one, she knew, had to be good. The *bandidos* up there had to be taken out permanently without a sound escaping from their lips, and that wouldn't be easy.

A badly wounded man tends to set up a terrible howl. They would have to be dead before they hit the ground. All three of them. Jessica had her knife in her hand. She didn't remember unsheathing it, but there it was, gleaming coldly in the night.

Ki touched her shoulder and made a motion. The gesture was emphatic: *Stay here*. Then Ki was gone, moving off into the shadows to their left. Jessica Starbuck could only lie there and watch the *bandidos.* listening to their muttered conversation.

"Get it over with," one of them said. "Hell, the peons will run like sheep."

"Yesterday they didn't."

"Yesterday Don Alejandro made a stupid error. He should have—"

Jessica didn't hear the rest of it, her mind had caught onto that one point and clung to it. Don Alejandro was here! Kurt Brecht himself had come with the reinforcements. The cartel general was in town somewhere, and if he could be found and killed, the slave running along the border could be broken.

Where was he? The cantina, of course. If she could tell Ki . . .

"It's getting damn cold," one of the bandits said. "Why don't we—"

"What?"

The bandit didn't respond. He fell face to the ground, dead, an arrow through his heart. The second bandit whirled, bringing his gun up. If he fired, it was all over. He didn't get the chance to pull the trigger, however; a *shuriken* whispered death through the air, striking the *bandido's* throat with deadly accuracy, and gagging and flailing, he toppled.

A third man took to his heels, but another arrow from Fly Catcher's vengeful bow took him down silently. Jessica snatched up the heavy kerosene cans and staggered out of the gully to the back of the building where the dead men lay.

Ki was already there, and as Jessie arrived, he took the kerosene and splashed it on the walls and the log eaves of the building.

"Ki," she whispered, "he's here. Don Alejandro is here."

"We can't do anything about it now."

"We can go after him," Jessica Starbuck said. Ki turned

to look at her, kerosene can in his hands. Starlight was in her blond hair. Her lips were parted with eagerness.

"No," was all Ki said.

"Ki, please. We can end it all with one stroke!" Her voice rose dangerously.

"It won't save the people of San Ignacio," Ki replied, and he was right, Jessica knew. Damn all, he was right. Mono would fight on. Killing Don Alejandro wouldn't save the town.

Fly Catcher stood by, silently watching as Ki worked. He took one of the cans and moved up a nearby alley, testing the wind by turning until it caressed his cheek. Yes, the Papago decided, this fire would sweep through San Ignacio, killing many if they were lucky.

Jessie and Ki darted across the street and began splashing kerosene on the buildings there. One of them was Fernando's barber shop. The next was the town hall. If the people of San Ignacio could have seen them then, they would have had trouble deciding who was the enemy, the *bandidos* or these strangers from the north.

A *bandido* appeared from nowhere, directly in front of Jessica and Ki, who were pouring kerosene onto a pile of wood beside the town hall.

There wasn't time for Ki to react and his hands were busy, but Jessica moved. Seeing the *bandido* draw his holstered gun, she threw her knife at him with deadly accuracy. Ki had spent hours showing her how to use a knife and now that training had paid off.

The knife struck heart muscle, and the bandit staggered back, already dead. The gun in his hand exploded with flame and noise, and Ki stiffened, looking at Jessica with anxious eyes.

"That does it," he said. "We will go. Now!"

"We haven't finished—"

"Now!"

From up the street they could already hear shouts, running feet, broken glass. Jessica took her box of matches from her pocket and struck one. The side of the town hall went up in a roar of red flame and smoke leaping to the skies.

They retreated up the alley, pausing to set the barber shop on fire. The flames crackled and came to thunderous life. Rounding the corner, they could see *bandidos* rushing toward them. Someone shouted and a finger pointed. They ran on, reaching the shelter of a building as a dozen shots rang out.

Fly Catcher had started three fires up a second alley. The flames leaped skyward, licking at the darkness. Ki used another match on the first building they had doused, and then with Fly Catcher on their heels, they raced for the gully.

San Ignacio was ablaze with light. Flames forty feet high painted smoky images against the night. The sound was tremendous. They never even heard the rifle shot that killed Fly Catcher.

The Indian was running beside them and he simply crumpled up as if every nerve in his body had been destroyed by the .44 slug that had ripped through his skull.

He went down and Jessica stopped to help him. Ki grabbed her arm, yanking her away.

"He's hurt," Jessie shouted.

Ki had had a better look. The top of the Papago Indian's skull was missing. "He's dead. Run or we will be, too."

Jessie glanced back and then followed Ki up the gully toward the mission. Shots rang in their ears. Once Jessica went down, ripping open a knee on a rock, but Ki lifted her to her feet, and they ran on, Jessie hobbling and in pain. Behind them, the guns died down and the flames increased.

It didn't help when one wild shot was cut loose by someone on the mission wall. Fortunately, there was only the one. If panic had set in and the guns along the parapet had opened up in unison, there was every chance that Jessie and Ki would have been killed.

Diego met them at the side gate. "Damn fool," he said. "I told everyone to watch what they were shooting at. He just wasn't listening."

"You didn't tell them we set the fire."

"No. We'd have a mutiny on our hands. Told them it was reconnaissance."

"Ki!" Maria was there suddenly and in Ki's arms.

"How did it—" Diego started to ask, but a cry from the wall aborted his question.

"Here they come! It's Mono!"

Ki held Maria's arms for a minute, looking up in disbelief at the sentry. Mono was coming again, now? Ki had expected stealth and care, but if they had already spotted Mono it meant a full-scale attack.

"You seem to have angered him," Diego said dryly.

Jessica commented, "Let's try to get him a little angrier then. He's making a mistake."

"Maybe," Ki said cautiously, "maybe Mono is making a great mistake."

On the other hand, maybe Mono was right. Maybe hurling all of his force against the mission from out of the night would be enough to send the peons into panic. Both sides recognized Mono's superiority of arms. Every shot of the Mexicans on the wall would have to count, whereas Mono's men could burn rounds of ammunition keeping the sentries' heads down while they stormed the walls.

"Let's get up there," Ki said. "Quickly."

Diego hesitated, still looking at the gate. "Where's the Indian? Where's Fly Catcher?" When they told him, he was silent before saying, "I'll get Don Alejandro for him. I swear it."

There wasn't time to worry about vengeance just then, however; survival was the only matter of importance. After climbing to the top of the thick walls, Ki and

Jessie were in time to see the first charge of Mono's *bandidos*.

Darkness covered much of their movement, and when the bandit force did appear, it was much closer than Ki had expected. They must have ridden to the mission, but now they had wisely abandoned their horses and were charging on foot toward the front gate.

"Let them have it!" Ki shouted and a barrage of musket fire cut down some in the front ranks of the onrushing *bandidos*. "Don't fire all at once! One rank at a time. Fire and then reload. Take your time when you aim!"

They didn't hear half of it and Ki had told them all of that before. It didn't seem to be doing much good. The Mexicans weren't disciplined soldiers. They were scared men fighting for their lives.

"The gate," Jessie shouted, and Ki ran that way along the top of the wall, risking a sniper's bullet. The bandits had dragged a heavy pole with them, and now they were using it as a battering ram. The thud of each impact could be felt along the wall.

Brother Joseph was there, his face lighted by the fires burning hotly beneath his ancient iron pots. Inside them, the olive oil was burbling, smoking, moving with heat.

The outlaws crashed into the gate again and the friar looked skyward.

"Pray later," Ki said, "fight now."

The friar crossed himself and bent to help Ki. They dumped the scalding oil onto the *bandidos* below, searing flesh and hair. With screams of pain and cries of terror, the outlaws fell back, the oil clinging to their flesh.

A second pot was overturned and the *bandidos* abandoned the battering ram in order to limp and dart back across the dark grass toward shelter. Musket balls took half of the unarmed *bandidos* down. One lay crying to the night for fifteen minutes before his pain was ended by death.

The field was silent.

"They retreated," Jessie said, wanting to believe it.

"Yes," Ki said thoughtfully. Then he realized what must be happening. "They won't try the front wall again. Every third man stay here! The rest of you to the side walls!" He cupped his hands to his mouth and repeated the command until they heard him and moved off along the wall to the north and south.

It was none too soon. From out of the night, the bandit guns spoke again and Mono charged the mission from the flanks, his repeating weapons laying down a screen of deadly fire.

A Mexican tumbled from the wall; another turned, his face shot away, and toppled toward the courtyard. Ki snatched up a musket, loaded it, and shot a charging bandit down.

The fire from San Ignacio still blazed and the bandits were clearly visible as they charged from the flanks now.

"Ki!" It was Jessie who first saw what the *bandidos* intended to do. Jessie called out to Ki. Moving through the gunsmoke and hail of bullets, Ki, too, saw it and he cursed.

Mono's's men had lashed poles together to form crude ladders. There were a dozen or more of them, and now as the people of San Ignacio spread out to try fighting back, Mono's primary attack concentrated itself once more on the front wall.

Rifle fire kept the heads of the men on the wall down as the bandits rushed the wall, setting up their ladders.

"Keep them back," Ki shouted.

The first enthusiastic volunteer tried to do just that and was shot through the guts for his trouble. Withering rifle fire from *bandidos* hidden in the darkness sent a hail of lead screaming toward the mission wall, blowing puffs of plaster and brick into the air and ricocheting wildly off the wall and metal pots, and striking the huge bell in the tower.

"Ki!" Jessie looked a frantic question at him.

"Hold them. Hold them for five minutes, just five minutes!" Ki shouted. "Brother Joseph!"

"Yes, Ki." The friar's eyes were wide but determined.

"The cellars, quickly. Now!"

"But why?"

"Now!"

The bandits were climbing the walls and being fought back. Musket fire answered the chatter of the constant Winchester shots. Ki raced toward the cellars, the friar behind him, his robes hiked high.

"These," Ki said, pointing out what he wanted.

"What good will they do?" the friar asked.

Ki gestured again and said more angrily than he intended, "Grab a couple of those cans, damn you, and do it now!"

Outside, the fire blazed red and orange against the sky, the shouts of the combatants mingled with the screams of the injured. From below, Ki saw a Mexican trigger his musket off into the face of a bandit who had just achieved the top of the wall. The man's face was washed away in a mask of gore.

Arturo would ride down no more children.

Diego was there, rifle in hands, face blackened by smoke and hair hanging into his handsome face. "What the hell are you doing to do, Ki?" he asked in astonishment.

"Fight! Get our people off the front wall. Have everyone pull back to the inner fortifications. The bell tower. And for God's sake get Jessica off that wall!"

The friar's face was as horrified as Diego's had been. He watched as Ki place the barrels of black powder they had carried up from the cellars along the base of the walal. It was the old powder, unstable and caked, very unreliable.

"I don't know if I want this to work or not to work," Brother Joseph said. "If it goes up, there won't be much of the mission left."

"If it doesn't," Ki said from where he was constructing crude fuses of cloth and gun powder, "there won't be any people left to come to the mission church. Hurry now—get back to the bell tower. Now!"

The friar left, reluctantly at first and then hurriedly. He waved his arm and shouted to the men along the wall. The *bandidos* had taken control of the wall. There wasn't a chance at all of holding it now.

Ki looked up, seeing a single peon left, fighting valiantly—Rivera, the alcalde. Then Rivera was shot down and Ki lit the fuses to his kegs and dashed toward the tower.

The short fuse hissed and sputtered, stammering their way toward the ancient powder. When they reached home, the black powder went up with a flash and a thunderous detonation that hurled Ki to the ground. He glanced back to see the wall go, to see the *bandidos* hurled into the air. Others were crushed beneath the weight of the wall. He staggered on, holding a bruised hip.

Leaping the barricades, he climbed the bell tower to where Jessie, Maria, Diego, and the friar stood, watching in awe as the cloud of smoke and dust rose high into the sky.

San Ignacio burned. The mission was nearly destroyed. And the battle had barely begun.

Chapter 17

Ki was exhausted. He crouched against the wall of the parapet around the bell tower, staring eastward and bleary-eyed at the rosy dawn rising and coloring the skies like a bloody memory.

Below them, the wall lay in ruins, and scattered across the courtyard and the field beyond were the bodies of the battle casualties.

Jessie, curled into a ball, slept beside Ki. Maria could not sleep, and so she stood, arms folded and black shawl over her shoulders, looking out over the ruins of the mission, of San Ignacio, of a way of life.

Brother Joseph appeared to be in shock. The friar walked the parapet, lips moving soundlessly, staring at the devastation.

The raiders came again an hour later. Along the parapet the weary defenders began to fire, reloading with painful slowness and answering ten of the *bandidos'* shots with one of their own. The bandits were fewer now, but even if the numbers had been the same, the outlaws would have had the advantage. All Ki and Jessie's army had going for them was position—and how long could they hold out on the bell tower with limited food and limited ammunition?

"No way out," Diego said putting it concisely. "They'll wear us down in the end."

The second night attack was beaten off. Mono seemed only half-hearted about the attempt. The *bandidos* out there settled into an unnerving sniping that went on the rest of the night. Bullets crashed into the tower, sometimes striking one of the bells and sometimes catching flesh.

Ki tried hard to keep everyone's spirits up. "They can't get us out of here," he told them. "Just hold out." Maybe a few of the more ignorant actually believed him.

"Something like your Alamo, eh?" Diego said.

"Something like it."

"Let's hope it doesn't end the same."

Jessica Starbuck, still managing to look beautiful despite the long battle, the gunsmoke on her face, and her tangled honey-blond hair, said, "It will end the same if we stay here, won't it, Ki?"

"I wouldn't say so."

"You can say it." She looked around. "There are only three of us here. If we stay here, we die sooner or later."

"So it would seem."

"Then," Jessie said, "we have to move, don't we?"

"We can't move," Diego said.

"Why not? The *bandidos* have mobility—we have none. If we don't move, we lose; you both admit that. Therefore, we have to move," she said.

"Sneak out," Diego said with distaste, "and run to the hills?"

"Run, hell," the blonde said with passion, "attack!"

Diego and Ki looked at each other in the darkness. The suggestion was absurd. Or was it?

"There's a handful of snipers out there," Jessica went on. "Where are the rest of the *bandidos?* Sleeping more than likely. Resting for a final assault in the morning. And how can we fight them back again? Sorry, my father was a practical man and just a little of that has rubbed off on me. We can't beat them back—not again. We only have one other option. We attack."

"The logic is impeccable," Diego Cardero said, "but as a practical woman, you know it's impossible."

"I said my father was practical, but damn all, he was also bold. When there's nothing left to do, when everything has to be won or lost on a single roll of the dice—damn it, you roll 'em!"

"Of course," Diego said, "you have an idea of how to go about this escapade."

"I have a thought or two. If either will work, I don't know. I know what happens if we stay here, though, and I don't like it, do you?"

"No," Cardero said, dropping his bantering tone, "I don't like it either, Jessica."

"What are you thinking?" Ki asked, looking down the parapet at his soldiers, some of whom slept with their backs to the wall.

"First the snipers. Likely they are the only sentries out. Why would Mono and Don Alejandro need any others?"

"You intend to find the snipers?" Cardero was incredulous, but apparently ready to go along with the madness now. "How?"

"Simplest thing in the world as long as they keep firing, isn't it?" Jessica responded.

"Simple, maybe. Just watch the muzzle flashes," Cardero commented, "but then what?"

"Then," Jessie said with her own brand of logic, "Ki will take care of them."

Cardero started to laugh, but Ki was thoughtful. As he looked out over the open ground between them and the burned town, a sniper did fire. He marked the position—it was unlikely the man would move. The sniper would have chosen what he thought was good cover, taken his canteen and perhaps a bottle with him, and settled in for the night's harmless fun of sniping at the

Mexicans in the tower, keeping their nerves on edge, keeping them from sleeping before the next attack, and tagging one now and them.

"Then what, Jessica?" Ki asked quietly. "Suppose it can be done? What do we do after that?"

She answered, "Got any of that powder left?"

Ki and Diego exchanged a glance. "Some," Ki replied. "Enough to keep our muzzle loaders in action for another day."

"Or," the blonde suggested, "enough to make one last whopping explosion. Right down Don Alejandro's throat."

Nobody but Jessie was high on the plan, but she hammered at them until they admitted there wasn't any real alternative. If they didn't strike quickly that very night and strike decisively, there was every chance they would die, that every single man, woman, and child in the mission would die, that Mono would continue his depredations, that the cartel under Don Alejandro, as Brecht was calling himself, would continue.

No one liked the plan, but they decided to go ahead with it. Diego began making fuses. Jessie heard him mutter, "This better work. I'm down to my last cigar."

Ki was also preparing himself to go out onto the plain and take out the snipers. For an hour he crouched behind the parapet, watching and at times rising and moving around intentionally drawing their fire. In the end he announced, "Five of them—I hope. Two in the gully, two to the south near that knoll, and one in the broken trees near the town."

"You can see the camp, can't you?" Jessica asked and Ki nodded.

He could see Mono's camp, the camp of Don Alejandro—north of town, not far from the river where a bluff crumbled away. A small fire burned and that meant only one thing: The *bandidos* had made their night camp there.

"Sorry, Ki, if I've gotten you into something you don't like," Jessie said, touching his arm briefly.

There was no need for apologies, no time to reconsider. Ki began to work his way toward the staircase, to move down into the night in his monk's robes. Maria was there at the head of the stairs.

"You are going out?" she asked. She bit her lower lip anxiously.

"Yes."

Then there was nothing to say. Her hands rested on his shoulders and fell away after a light, meaningful kiss, and Ki was on his way.

The first one couldn't have been much easier. Ki found the sentry sleeping, a bottle propped up on his chest between his brown, gnarled hands. He never woke up as Ki applied pressure to the carotid arteries and slowly starved the brain of its blood. Ki took the man's Winchester and moved on, a dark, shadowy thing in the gully. The moon glossed the open land, shadowed the depressions deeply. The second sentry was wide awake and sober.

It didn't do him any good. Ki was a wraith, and as the startled guard brought up the knife he drew from his belt sheath, Ki blocked the thrust. His wrists crossed to catch the Mexican's wrist, deftly grabbing the arm and twisting. With the sentry off balance, Ki's knee smashed into his face, and he fell back, unconscious or dead—Ki didn't care which.

The next one was more of a problem. Alone in a small depression, he was surrounded by open ground. There was no way even Ki was going to approach unseen. As Ki, huddled in the gully, watched, the sniper fired twice at the bell tower. A bronze bell rang distantly and the reaction of the sniper's body seemed to express satisfaction. He got to his knees and peered toward the mission.

The *shuriken* was a soundless thing, whispering deadly

threats as it spun from Ki's hand and caught the sniper in the eye. The man pawed at the throwing star and then collapsed.

Ki moved on, after taking that one's rifle as well. He glanced at the moon—how much time before dawn? How much time before Mono and his cartel boss decided to attack again?

The other two were awake but not alert. They were playing cards, drinking, and apparently only now and then rising to take a shot at the bell tower.

They took no more shots as Ki leaped between them, scattering cards and silver money. The narrow, scarred Mexican leaped up, trying to escape from Ki's onslaught. He couldn't escape, couldn't dodge the blow that Ki drove into the *bandido*'s heart, stopping it immediately.

The other man was Halcón.

He had a pistol in his hand. Halcón was smiling, sure he had won. Ki, apparently surprised defenseless, had already planned his move against Halcón. Turning, he slapped out with his left hand, a seemingly futile and soft gesture, but the gun went flying as Halcón grabbed his broken wrist. Enraged, the Indian charged blindly. Ki's staggering blow stopped the bandit in his tracks, and as Halcón tried to fight back, Ki finished him with a middle-knuckle blow, a strike to the center of Halcón's forehead. Bone crushed beneath the master's hand, and the bandit, waving his hand uselessly, reflexively, went down to lie beside his dead companion.

Ki picked up the two Winchesters and started on, still glancing at the moon, counting the minutes, seconds. The low campfire burned ahead, dark against the willow-clotted river, and Ki looked to the knoll above it. Had Jessie and Diego made it? Was any of this going to work?

A bandit sentry appeared to Ki's right and he went to the ground, not wanting to risk another confrontation now that he was this close.

The wait was interminable as the sentry rolled a cigarette, muttered to himself, turned around, and walked back along the river toward the camp.

The sky was paling and Ki watched it anxiously, knowing that with the dawn the *bandidos* would be up and moving, knowing that without the night to cover his movements he had no chance at all.

He moved through the brush, smelling the damp sage and the river beyond, then climbing the sandy knoll to come face to face with a man and a Colt revolver.

"Jesus," Diego Cardero rasped, lowering his weapon, "you can be too damned quiet, you know."

Diego helped Ki up and together they walked to where Jessica Starbuck waited with her two barrels of black powder.

"Where have you been?" she asked Ki.

"Train was late."

"They're starting to stir," she whispered, and Ki peered downward, seeing the men in the bandit camp—some still asleep in their blankets, others gathering around the fire for morning coffee.

"Preparing for the slaughter?" Diego asked.

"Yes." Jessie was impatient, and she was right. Do it now, before they were fully awake, before they were alert and ready to fight, before some chance movement, some casual glance toward the knoll, could give away the plan.

"Now," Ki said, "light the fuses."

★

Chapter 18

Jessie struck the first match and touched it to the crude rag fuse. Crude it might have been, but it worked. A sparkling, sputtering serpent writhed toward the can of black powder, and Jessica Starbuck rolled it down the bluff into the heart of the outlaw camp.

Heads lifted curiously. Then the *bandidos* leaped into panicky motion, diving toward cover.

It didn't do most of them any good. Five pounds of black powder went up with a flash and boom like a mountain thunderstorm. Ki and Diego opened up with their repeating rifles, picking off the fleeing outlaws. The second keg of gunpowder followed the first and the detonation killed a dozen men, tearing bodies apart and flinging them into the willows.

Horses bolted, The *bandidos,* many of them still uncertain as to what had happened and wandering aimlessly around the camp, were easy targets for the merciless Winchesters.

Through the screen of rising smoke, beyond the chaos of the camp, Ki saw the man he wanted. Mono, wildly gesturing, pistol in hand, was urging his men to take the knoll.

There wasn't a chance in hell of that as bandit after bandit went down before the rifles fired from above, fired until their barrels were red hot.

Mono took to his heels, and Ki saw his objective—the big bay horse apparently dazed and standing in the willows, already saddled, its reins trailing. Ki tried one shot; he missed as the bullet clipped brush beside Mono's head, and then he dropped the hammer of an empty chamber.

Mono was on his horse, riding northward, and Ki got to his feet.

"Ki!" Jessie cried, but there was no stopping him. He tossed his repeater to Jessica.

"Reload this and use it."

Before Jessica Starbuck could respond, Ki was off at a run, following the bearded, maniacal bandit leader northward.

He ran easily, weaving through the tall willow brush with his heart pounding heavily but steadily in his chest. Mono was there ahead of him. The bandit turned in the saddle and emptied his Colt wildly in Ki's direction. Ki never slowed down. He ran on, splashing across the wide, shallow river to cut off Mono's escape.

Mono was riding hard, following the river. He was there and then he wasn't. Suddenly the land was empty; the distant shots Jessica and Diego fired were the only sounds.

Ki crouched, waiting and listening. A horse nickered and he lifted his head.

Mono charged out of the brush, trying to ride Ki down. Ki flung himself to one side, reaching out and grasping at Mono's leg. All he caught was stirrup and he held to that grimly as Mono kicked at him viciously and rode the horse into the stream.

The horse's right foreleg buckled as it found a hole in the river bottom, and Mono was thrown as the big bay rolled. The thrashing hooves of the frantic animal narrowly missed Ki's head and he dived under, coming up to face Mono who still had his Colt in his hand.

Ki kicked, driving the revolver from Mono's hand, and the bearded giant roared, while coming in and wildly thrashing his arms and winging his massive fists at Ki's head.

It was no contest. Mono with a gun was one thing; Mono alone was another. A single punch to the bandit king's chest stopped him cold. He clutched his chest and fell back, gasping for breath.

Mono sank into the water, still trying to fill his empty lungs with air, but there was only water there, cool, blue water, and it flowed into his mouth, flooding his lungs. Mono kicked and gasped and then sank a little in the river, floating slowly away downstream, his dead eyes open to the willows and the crimson sunrise.

Ki started to jog back toward the bandit camp.

Jessica had emptied her carbine again. Below was destruction and death, but she didn't feel the slightest pity for these men who had come to kill, to burn, to enslave.

"Here," Diego said, nudging her, and Jessica took a handful of cartridges from him and automatically reloaded, although there seemed to be few living targets below.

"Do you see him?" Jessica asked.

"Don Alejandro?"

"Yes. He was right there; now he's gone."

Diego Cardero peered into the sunlight, searching the battlefield below. Somehow the man had disappeared. In the smoke and confusion, he had made his way out of the camp apparently. But to where? Cardero's eyes caught the sudden flash of movement in the willows and he shouted.

"There!" he said, his finger pointing beyond the ravaged camp to where Brecht was trying to make his escape.

Jessica lifted her rifle to her shoulder, realized she didn't have a shot, and lowered it again. Then she was off, sprinting down the sandy bluff toward the outlaw camp, ignoring Diego's shouted warnings.

She reached the willows on a dead run and started fighting her way through the brush. He had to be stopped. To come this near and then allow Brecht to escape was unthinkable. Jessie paused, listening to the hum of the insects in the brush along the river. Then she heard the sound of hoofbeats, saw the sudden blur of movement beyond the screen of silver willows, and darted that way, rifle in hand.

She reached the river in time to see Brecht splashing across it on a roan horse. Jessica lifted her rifle, fired twice, and missed as the running horse achieved the far side of the river and disappeared into the brush and oaks.

A second horse stood not far to the north, tied to a broken oak and tossing its head in annoyance or fear. Jessie ran that way, swung aboard the skittish animal, and heeled it sharply toward the river.

They splashed across, silver fans of water flying from the roan's hooves and started on after Brecht who had a good half mile lead by now.

The burned town was to Jessie's left, the endless desert to her right. Brecht was straight ahead of her, riding toward the south, toward his ranch and safety.

Jessie tried a shot, but from the back of the galloping horse it was a chancy thing for even such a marksman as she was, and the bullet flew wide. Brecht seemed to be unarmed. She saw him turn in the saddle as her shot winged its way past his head, saw him duck low and urge his roan horse into the sandy foothills below San Ignacio. Then the roan found a squirrel hole with its right front hoof, and Jessica saw nothing else as the roan went down, rolling and tumbling with its hooves thrashing at the air and a cloud of sand dust flying.

Something rose up to thump solidly against Jessie's

head, and the sun went cold and dark as she fell spinning into a vasty empty cavern.

When she came to, Diego and Ki were there. Both men looked concerned, but both smiled as she shook her head, held her skull, and sat up.

"Sit still, Jessica," Ki said. His hands were on her shoulders, pressing her down.

"Brecht—"

"He's gone, I'm afraid, long gone now."

Diego handed Jessica a canteen and she drank from it. Not far from her the roan lay dead.

Jessica drank from the canteen, letting the water trickle down her throat. The humming cleared from her brain, and the flashing lights behind her eyes dissolved. "I almost had him," she said.

"Almost," Diego answered. He smiled but that did nothing to dispell the gloom and anger inside Jessica Starbuck.

"Damn all, I almost had him!" She looked at Ki, "You're back—you got Mono."

"I got Mono," Ki responded. He and Diego had Jessica by her arms now, hoisting her to her feet. She stood there woozily for a while and then shook free of them to turn and stare southward, southward toward Alejandro's path of retreat.

Slowly then she turned back, and the three of them started walking toward the ravaged town where smoke still billowed into the air. Beyond the town the church lifted its ruined bell tower against the pale blue sky.

Brother Joseph was at the battered mission gate to meet them. Maria rushed into Ki's arms. In the mission yard itself, the people of San Ignacio had begun an impromptu fiesta. The town mariachi played. They all danced—weary, smoke-blackened peasants relieved suddenly of their burden, of the fear of death.

Inside the church Brother Joseph sent for water and towels. Jessica and the men cleaned up as well as possible. When Jessie glanced at the friar, she saw his head bowed and his hands clasped, and she heard him saying a prayer of thanksgiving.

"It is done," the friar said aloud finally, his face beaming.

Jessica Starbuck disagreed. "It's not done at all."

"Why," he said, "what can you mean? Mono is gone; the bandits are gone or dead. We have won."

"We've won," Diego Cardero said darkly, "but Don Alejandro has escaped. He's alive yet to organize more *bandido* gangs to ride out and take more Indian slaves."

"I realize this," the friar said, "but what more can we do? The *federales* will be informed and they will put an end to Don Alejandro's slaving."

"By the time the *federales* can do anything, Brecht will be gone again. Maybe he won't be able to run his slave operation in this area anymore, but he'll be out there doing something just as nasty."

"He still holds slaves," Ki said worriedly.

"What do you mean?" the friar asked.

Jessica told him, "He won't be able to run with them. If he has to flee, he may take it into his head to kill them."

"But that is maniacal."

"Not in Brecht's mind, not in the minds of those who control him. It's simply good business," Ki said coldly.

"But I can't believe..." The friar had hardly led a sheltered life. He'd seen enough to know what goes on in the world, but this was something beyond his understanding.

"Fly Catcher," Jessica said quietly.

"The Indian—but he is dead."

"He's dead, and Ki and I would likely be dead if he hadn't taken a hand when he did."

Diego Cardero said, "I took an oath that I would see Don Alejandro dead. I promised this to Fly Catcher. I promised this to my mother."

"We're going to do it," Jessica Starbuck said firmly. She looked to Ki who nodded silently. "We're going to get the man. If there are any slaves being held in the Casa Alejandro, and I'd wager there are, we owe it to them."

The friar shook his head in disapproval. "You will all die as well. How can you attack a fortified position? Here we at least had the mission walls, a few tricks. The Alejandro place sits on a hill and is protected well. You would need an army to assault it."

Maria said. "We have an army."

"I don't understand," the bewildered friar answered.

"We have an army—if they'll fight. We have the people of San Ignacio."

"No," the friar said, "I forbid it!"

Maria's eyes met Brother Joseph's. She shook her head with sadness. "I respect you. I love the church. But this is something that you cannot forbid. It is something that must be done. There is a debt owed and the people of San Ignacio must pay it. There is more than one way to lose your soul, and if our people cannot help now, will not fight now, then surely their souls are lost."

Ki touched the girl's shoulder, "Maria," he began to say, "if—"

"It must be this way. Come with me or stay. I am going to speak to the people, to my neighbors and relatives and friends." There wasn't any stopping her. She marched purposefully toward the door and, after at last backward glance, went out to the crowded churchyard.

Jessica Starbuck was smiling. "Well," she said to Ki, "I suppose we'd better follow this stubborn woman of yours." Ki smiled and followed along, leaving the friar to his praying.

Outside, the dancing continued. Maria walked through the twirling dancers to the spot where the band stood playing. Her hand placed across the bridge of a guitar brought the music to an awkward halt, and the people of San Ignacio turned toward her, curious, wary, or simply confused.

Maria waited until the barrage of questions quieted down, until the churchyard, bathed in white sunlight and dusty and smoke-scented, had become silent.

One person shouted, "What are you doing, Maria? Let us dance."

"You dance while people live in chains," the Mexican woman replied. She put her hands on her hips and leaned slightly forward, her tone scolding. "You dance while the enemy of our people runs to the safety of his fortress."

Jessie and Ki had come up behind Maria; Diego Cardero stood beside them, silently observing. In the window above them Brother Joseph stood watching silently. A hot dry wind drifted dust across the churchyard.

"What are you talking about Maria? The *bandidos* have been defeated; the battle has been won. Let us dance for a little while, sing a bit. Let us celebrate what we have done."

"Celebrate!" Maria spat out the word. "You celebrate while those who saved San Ignacio prepare to go into battle." She gestured toward Jessie and Ki and toward a darkly smiling Diego Cardero.

"Tell us what you are talking about, Maria Sanchez."

And she did. "Mono was a snake, but a snake set free by this man called Don Alejandro, nurtured by him, protected by him. Don Alejandro takes slaves from the Indian tribes and brings them south—something we have allowed by ignoring it, something we have encouraged with out fear of the slavers, or men like Mono.

"When Mono turned on San Ignacio, these three saved us—these three who should have cared nothing for our town. Yet they fought for us. Now Mono is dead. Mono is dead, but his master lives on. And you," she said mockingly, "you would let three alone go against this desert wolf, this Don Alejandro."

"What can we do, Maria?" a man asked.

"You can fight!"

"Fight again?" the Mexican said. "Fight with what? Fight for what cause? For San Ignacio we would fight, but what is this war about? We have families, we have—"

"You have your soft beds and your fat bellies to think of!" Maria Sanchez shot back. "I know all of this. But, my friends, you should think of your honor. You owe these people a debt of honor. You owe your souls such a debt. Stay here and dance," she said, suddenly turning her back to the people, "or be men."

It worked. The appeal to their manhood, to their pride, brought the men forward slowly. They asked, "What can we do? Where can we get weapons?"

Ki told them, "The dead are out there—the dead who wanted to kill you, who may one day be replaced by others who will want the same. The *bandidos* were armed. Let us arm ourselves now—those of you who will fight. Let's arm ourselves and march south before it's too late, before Don Alejandro has killed people like you—people who only want to live, to sing, to dance in the sun."

Chapter 19

It was a ragged looking, uncertain army, but it was the best Jessie and Ki had. They moved out of San Ignacio at sunrise and started south, south toward Don Alejandro's fortress.

Maria rode beside Ki—there was no keeping the Mexican woman behind. She had a Winchester repeater slung over her shoulder; her hair was knotted at the base of her neck. Maria would fight and she, more than Jessie and Ki, knew what they were getting into.

"Once," she said, "I saw his place. It sits atop a bluff surrounded by rocks and thickets of nopal cactus. There is only one road approaching it."

"We'll have to give that some thought," Ki said.

"Give it much thought, Ki," she suggested. "Also, we have not seen the end of Don Alejandro's bandit army yet. Some of them must have been left behind to watch the slaves and to guard the house. I once told you Mono could gather an army of a hundred men if need be. How many would you guess Don Alejandro can count on?"

Ki glanced at Jessica and then looked to their own army, which trailed along behind them, carrying their weapons in all positions. It had been difficult enough to get them to fight for their own town—what were they going to do when the shooting started now?

"We've started walking down this road," Jessica Starbuck said. "We can't turn back now."

"No," Ki answered, "we can't turn back. But I don't have to enjoy the idea, Jessica."

By late afternoon they were in sight of the house. It was an imposing sight perched atop the apparently insurmountable bluff. It had two stories of plastered adobe capped by a red tiled roof; two towers had been incorporated into the design. These overviewed the flats below where Jessie and Ki now lay prone, searching the desert valley.

"There's no way to get across the flats unseen," Diego Cardero said gloomily. He shaded his eyes against the sun and shook his head as he studied the layout again.

"It will have to be after dark," Jessica said, and both men glanced at her.

"We can't attack in darkness, Jessica," Diego answered. "We would be lucky to find the road. If we did find it, we would find guards there. It's impossible to climb the bluff itself through that cactus." He looked to Ki for agreement, but Ki wouldn't commit himself just yet.

"There aren't many options, Ki," Jessie said. She had removed her hat, and now she ran a hand across her forehead, bringing it away streaked with dust.

"Maybe one other," Ki replied. He was looking not across the flats toward the house itself, but eastward where a slow procession was making its way toward them.

"What's that?" Diego asked. No one answered. In another minute it was obvious what he was seeing. Ox carts and walking people. Men and women afoot, children in the carts. They were being watched by outriders. "Slaves. Slaves arriving at the ranch." He said it with extreme bitterness. Diego hadn't forgotten that his own mother had been taken by these people, taken and killed.

"Why would they still be arriving here?" Maria asked.

"How would the slavers know anything about the trouble at San Ignacio? They are simply making their normal delivery."

"If we only knew that Brecht was still here," Jessica said.

Ki responded, "No matter—there are slaves there. I want Brecht as badly as you do, Jessie, but the Indians must be set free. And I think the slavers themselves have presented us with a way to do just that."

"What are you thinking of, Ki?"

"Using the slave caravan to get into the ranch," he answered.

"It can't be done!" Diego said.

"We don't know that," Ki said with a soft smile. "We haven't tried it yet. But we will. I don't see an alternative."

"They'd hear any shots from the ranch," Maria said.

"Then it will have to be done in silence. In dead silence."

They started to work their way down the hill to where their army waited. Jessie took Ki's arm briefly and, out of the hearing of the others, said, "Ki, I don't like this very much."

"No, neither do I. In fact," he added, "I don't much like anything that has happened to us since we crossed the border, but as you once said, 'We've started walking down this road. We can't turn back now.'"

Jessie had no answer for him. She let go of Ki's arm and walked with him to where the others anxiously waited. Ki waited until they had gathered around and then he told them exactly what had to be done.

The slave caravan moved slowly. The oxen pulling the carts were weary. The carts rocked and swayed and bounced over each rut and rock. Behind the carts the Indians, some of them in chains, walked, shuffling their feet.

The caravan was guarded by six men, six heavily armed *bandidos*, but they, too, had come a long way, they, too, were weary. As they wound their way through the deep, shadowed canyon, they didn't bother to glance up at the craggy ridges. They were nearly home, nearly back to the ranch where their beds, tequila, slave women awaited them. And gold. Much gold, for Don Alejandro paid well.

Ki had worked his way halfway down the brush slope above the narrow trail. Now he waited, holding his breath as the carts and plodding slaves passed him. He let one guard go by and then another. When the last man in line appeared around the bend in the trail, Ki reached into his pocket and withdrew a deadly, bright *shuriken*.

He scarcely changed position, but his body coiled, poising. He drew a leg under him, shifted his balance, and cocked his arm. Looking to his right where the bandits and their captives had lost themselves around a second bend, Ki waited.

One *bandido* was fat and sweaty and wore a black sombrero and black vaquero suit. He carried a shot gun and wore two pistols. Behind his saddle, half a dozen sets of manacles jangled softly. The *bandido* yawned and Ki's *shuriken* hissed savagely through the air to rip the throat from the fat man. He clutched once at the *shuriken* and then toppled heavily from the horse's back to lay dead against the dusty earth.

Ki scrambled down the slope, gesturing to the man behind him. The Mexican stumbled in his anxiousness but caught up with Ki. Ki ripped the clothing from the fat man and shoved it to him.

"Hurry," Ki prompted.

"If they find out I'm not one of them—" the Mexican objected.

"Do it, now! Or they will find out."

Ki watched briefly as the man from San Ignacio began

stripping off his own clothes; then he turned and sprinted softly after the slave caravan.

Ahead of Ki, Diego Cardero, knife in hand, lay in a gully beside the trail. He heard the riders slowly rounding the bend and the screech of ungreased wheels against wooden axles. He lowered his head, gripping the knife more tightly.

Diego peered up through the screen of chia and sage-brush, seeing a horseman pass—a narrow, scarred man riding a gray horse with silver trappings.

That was one man—Cardero counted them as they passed his position. If Ki had done his work, the fifth man would be the last. And Diego had no doubt that the Japanese had done his work. He had never seen a warrior to equal Ki.

Four *bandidos* had passed. The next one then. Diego watched closely; the slavers ahead hadn't yet cleared the bend. If they glanced back . . . The fifth slaver appeared, straggling now, glancing behind him, perhaps realizing that one man was missing. Diego could see the perplexed expression in his eyes, could see him holding up his horse a little as he looked back down the winding, narrow trail.

Slowly the bandit halted his horse and turned it. He shifted the rifle he held in his hand and sat his blue roan, waiting for the man behind him, the man who would not be coming.

Cardero raised himself cautiously and then launched himself from the underbrush, leaping for the back of the bandit's horse. He was up behind the *bandido* before the man knew what had happened, and Cardero, one hand over the slaver's mouth, stabbed deeply with his knife, ripping at heart muscle and lung tissue as the bandit thrashed futilely in his arms. The bandit fell from his horse, rifle dropping free and Cardero bent low to recover the man's sombrero.

Ki was jogging around the bend in the trail now, pointing ahead. Cardero nodded and turned his stolen horse. Behind Ki, the second masquerading attacker came. He seemed relieved to see Cardero, grinned, and held up the shotgun taken from the dead *bandido*. Diego nodded and they started on together.

Rata was what the pocked bandit was called. Rat—it suited him well. Rata was riding beside the last cart. Where were that stupid Domingo and the equally stupid Ramon? What use were those two? Stupid and lazy.

Even back at the Indian village, they had been useless. They didn't fight worth a damn when those braves had decided to try making a stand. They stood back and watched. Don Alejandro himself would hear about that!

Rata saw them coming—finally. The two of them towing a slave between them. Maybe Rata had been wrong. They had captured an escaping slave at least. That was a thousand pesos they had saved Don Alejandro.

When had the slave gotten away? Rata frowned and started his horse toward the two slavers. The man they held between them was tall, very tall. His head was down, but even so Rata could have sworn he had never seen this one before. Even his face was not Indian. Nor was it Mexican.

"Hey, Domingo! What is this? *Qué pasa?* Who have you got there?"

Rata's beady eyes narrowed. Something was not right. He held up his horse again. That wasn't Domingo at all!

That was the last coherent thought Rata was to have in his violent life. As he watched, the slave between the two horsemen freed his hands and then something silver and flashing was humming its way toward him, something that sailed like a dragonfly, seemingly insubstantial. It buried itself in Rata's forehead with a force like a mule's kick.

Rata lifted his gun, but his fingers could not hold the

rifle that was suddenly as heavy as an anvil. Rata watched his rifle fall to the ground. With a pawing gesture, he swiped at the thing imbedded in his forehead, and then he slid to the earth, his hand trying to hold his saddlehorn and was dragged a few feet by his horse.

From the brush, a man appeared, rushed to Rata's body, and began stripping it as Ki and Diego passed. The Mexican yanked the *shuriken* from Rata's forehead, glanced at it in wonder, and tossed it to Ki who caught it and tucked it away in his pocket.

Three. There should only be three of them left, Maria Sanchez thought, if everything had gone right. She was crouched in the tall, purple flowering sage beside the trail—listening, waiting, and watching. She let the first two riders pass her, watching them glance down across the valley and past the sheer drop that now sided the trail toward the Casa Don Alejandro.

She was silent and motionless, but when the third man appeared, she ripped open the seam of her riding blouse's sleeve and began to moan softly.

"Help me. *Por favor,* help me. In the name of God."

The slaver was almost past her when he heard her cries, saw Maria stagger up from the brush and then fall back in a faint. He turned his horse, swung down, and walked to her.

This was something. *Madre de Dios,* a beautiful woman alone in the country. Smiling, the bandit walked into the brush, moving toward Maria who lay face up, her breasts straining at the fabric of her light blouse. Three buttons were open and the glimpse of smooth, coppery cleavage the bandit caught caused his breath to strangle off to a hiss. He worked his way down the slope toward Maria.

He never saw the other woman, the honey-blonde with the green eyes who moved silently behind him and drove her knife into his back as he stood slavering over Maria

Sanchez, his body tightening with thoughts of what he could do with such a woman.

He never saw Jessica Starbuck, but he felt the razor-edged knife bit into his flesh, felt the sudden, jagged pain. He tried to turn, to fight off his assailant, but the woman on the ground suddenly rose up, slashing out with her own knife. The blade raked his throat, and then the bandit was aware of nothing else. He fell to the ground to die twitching.

Maria Sanchez spat into his dying face.

"Two left," Jessica said. "Let's hope they die as silently."

They did die silently. Quickly and silently. Diego rode by the line of carts, dragging a thrashing Ki by the collar. As the two lead *bandidos* turned to find out what was happening, Ki took the man on their left. Leaping from the ground, he took the bandit down by the throat, took him down and with a crushing blow to the man's throat, and left him strangling in the dust.

Diego had brought the rifle he carried up and around and, wielding it like a club, slammed it against the skull of the *bandido* to the right. He dropped from the horse in a tangle and rolled off into the brushy ravine below them.

And then there were none. Only the men of San Ignacio dressed in bandit clothes, the two women, Ki, and Diego—and half a hundred fearful, perplexed Indian slaves who stood or sat in the carts staring at these newcomers.

"What do we do with them?" Diego asked, dusting himself off.

"The slaves? We need them," Ki answered.

"We can't, Ki," Jessica interrupted, touching Ki's arm. "Look at them. How can we drag them on with us? They think they're still slaves. Let them go."

"If we let them go—"

"Our people can take their places. No one will notice the difference, not right away."

Ki looked again at the wretched Indians. Reluctantly he admitted that Jessica was right. "We'll let them go. Diego, are they Papago Indians? Can you talk to them?"

"I'll find out. These are not Papago. Maybe that one there," he gestured. "What do I tell them?"

"To run. To turn and run and don't look back. To go home and hide in the hills."

Diego found one old man who spoke many tongues. It was to him that Cardero gave the instructions. Even after the old man translated what Cardero had said, however, many of the Indians remained where they were, thinking perhaps it was a trick. It wasn't until Diego gave the old man a spare rifle and one of the Mexicans produced the key to the manacles that he found in the pocket of a jacket that a buzz of conversation and excited movement began.

"Tell them to keep quiet, Cardero. Just keep quiet and go."Ki looked to those who had filtered down through the brush to join them. "Start getting up into the carts. No hats, for God's sake. Keep your weapons hidden." Ki looked to the sky, seeing the sun start to drop toward the western mountains. "At dusk," he told them, "when it will be difficult for any guards to make us out—at dusk we attack."

They waited on the canyon trail, guards posted behind and ahead of the slave train. The Mexicans in the carts were unsettled, nervously watching the sun as it arced lower, flushed pink, and then vanished into the cradle of the dark mountains beyond the valley.

"They're nervous," Jessica said, "and I don't blame them. We could darn well be setting them up for a slaughter."

Ki had been watching the big house on the peak across the dark valley. His thoughts were much the same as

Jessie's, but it did no good now to reflect on them. He had seen little activity around the house—Once in a while a guard on the stony bluff above the cactus thicket, and once what seemed to be a man in the window of one of the towers. Other than that there was nothing, which meant that Brecht was probably still there. As far as Ki could tell, there was only one way in and one way out of the fortress, and no one had gone up or down it.

Ki turned suddenly. It was time. He glanced at the sun himself, tugged down the sombrero he wore, and nodded. Returning to the canyon trail, he swung aboard a gray horse with a silver mounted saddle and waited while the rest of his soldiers took their positions.

Jessie was beside him in a vaquero's suit that was far too big and showed a blood stain on the front. She looked silently at Ki, waiting. Her mouth was dry; her hand clenched the repeating rifle she held.

Ki's hand lifted and then fell and he started his horse forward. The carts with their human burden creaked into motion. The men of San Ignacio, posing as slaves, trudged forward, with their heads down and their pistols beneath their shirts. Diego Cardero looked skyward once, as if calling to an old Papago war spirit. Maria Sanchez, also in a man's clothing, breathed a word that might have been a prayer—or a curse.

They wound down the canyon trail, rolled onto the shadowy valley, and made their way toward the great house. It stood in sunlight still, although the rest of the knoll, the valley, and the lower surrounding hills were dark. No one spoke. There was no sound but the screeching of wheels, the occasional blowing of a horse, and the creak of saddle leather.

Cardero, who would do the talking, rode in front now, Ki beside him, and Jessie back a way so that her disguise wouldn't be so obvious.

They found the gate that shut off the road to the big house, opened it from on horseback, and rolled on through.

The road turned sharply upward and narrowed. Nopal cactus, shoulder high to a horse and impenetrable, clotted the bank above them.

"Here's trouble," Cardero whispered urgently and Ki, too, saw the men: two guards carrying shotguns standing across the road, blocking their progress.

One of them called out, "Fine time to show up, Rata."

"What's wrong?" Cardero answered in a hoarse voice. Ki saw one of the guards thumb back the hammers to his shotgun. The bluff wasn't going to work. A smooth, hard *shuriken* filled Ki's hand. The one on the right first if need be, he thought.

"We're pulling out. Everything's gone to hell . . . Rata?" the guard said questioningly. He came forward, peering at Cardero out of the deep dusk.

"Damn it all—who are you?" the guard demanded. He brought his shotgun up and cut loose a load of buckshot, the roar of it shattering the stillness of the night and ending the masquerade with blood and gunsmoke.

★

Chapter 20

The load of buckshot belched from the fiery muzzle of the shotgun carried by Don Alejandro's guard. Ki had already been moving as the guard brought the shotgun up, for he had thrown himself from horseback to roll to the side of the road, and from a kneeling position, he flipped a deadly *shuriken* into the throat of the guard. The second man acted too slowly to be of any help. A shot from Jessica's Winchester ripped through his body, slamming him back against the earth to twitch for a moment before dying painfully.

"Diego?" Ki called out.

"I'm all right, Diego Cardero answered. "You should see the hat I was wearing, though."

Maria wasn't nearly as calm as the two men. "They'll be coming now. That's done it!"

Ki was to his feet and dragging one of the guards to the side of the road. "Quickly roll them down into the cactus."

"What good will that—"

"Quickly," Ki snapped.

Diego took the other man and kicked him over the side. It wasn't a moment too soon. Three guards on foot were running down the trail, rifles at the ready. Ki adopted a casual stance and Diego followed suit, holding his rifle beside his leg. The guards, seeing no apparent trouble, slowed a little, their alertness dropping a notch.

"What's going on?" one of them demanded.

"Damn slave," Cardero muttered. "Bastard tried to take off—" He lifted a pointing finger and the guards' eyes automatically followed. "Through the damned nopal."

Something rang in one of the guard's heads. He realized something was wrong, although his reasoning hadn't yet identified it. He turned sharply, bringing his rifle up. Ki slamed the butt of his rifle into the guard's throat, and he collapsed like a sack of potatoes. The other two suddenly found themselves covered by three guns and they dropped their weapons warily, looking from Ki to Jessie to Diego.

"Tie them up and gag them. Tear one of those Indian blankets into strips," Diego ordered.

Ki stopped him, "Wait a minute. I want to talk to one of them." He stood near a tall guard with pouched eyes and a very frightened expression. "Where are the slaves?" he asked.

"Go to hell," the guard answered.

Ki lifted his hand and put it on the man's throat. Searching for and finding a knot of nerve endings he began to apply pressure, and excruciating pain shot through the guard's body. He wasn't brave enough to take that.

"Behind the house," he panted as Ki's hand continued its probe of the nerve endings. "They've dug a pit."

"A pit!" Maria gasped.

The guard wasn't aware enough of what was going on to be surprised by a woman's voice. Ki still held his grip, and now anger had tightened his fingers, anger at the guard, Don Alejandro, the cartel.

"What's the pit for?" Ki asked.

"To–to bury them. Don Alejandro is leaving. We can't take them with us . . . *Madre de Dios, señor!* The pain!"

Ki's hand fell away. "Tie this one, too," he said savagely. To the men of San Ignacio, he said, "Everyone out. Here—here's a rifle. You take this one."

"It is time to fight?" one of the peasants asked.

"You heard what they're going to do here," Ki responded angrily. "What do you think?"

"I think, *señor,*" the man answered, "that it is time to fight."

"Criminals," Maria muttered bitterly, "savages!"

"What's the plan, Ki?" Diego asked.

"There may not be time to worry about one," Ki answered. "There are two objectives—the house and the place of execution. Leave the house until last. We've got to stop them from killing those slaves. Leave the horses. Come on! Silently. Silently and swiftly."

Men filtered past Ki in the night. He couldn't see their faces, but he could feel their anger. Revulsion at Don Alejandro's savage plan had strengthened the backbones of the men of San Ignacio.

"Ki." Jessie was beside him.

Ki nodded. "Let's go. It's time our man paid the price."

They began to jog up the trail. Above them they could make out a single tower against the dark sky. Stars were beginning to blink on; the air was rich with the scent of nopal and sage. Ki's silent army moved through the shadows.

The night was dark and empty and quiet. The quiet lasted to the top of the road. There an iron gate with plenty of firepower protecting it stood in their way.

From behind the gate and adjacent stone wall, rifles opened up spitting flame into the night. A man went down in front of Ki, flinging his rifle away as he writhed in pain. Another crumpled up with a cry of anguish. Ki's army answered the *bandidos*' guns with a barrage of their own. Bullets whined off the stone wall and rang against iron.

Ki saw a *bandido* rise from behind the wall and be cut in half by a blast from a shotgun. Jessica was to Ki's right, and he glanced her way, assuring himself she was all right for the time being.

Ki never slowed as he reached the wall. He hurdled it, delivering a kick to the face of a guard and crushing his skull. Rolling to the ground, Ki swept the feet out from under a second man just as he was ready to fire with his Colt pistol.

Ki chopped at the side of the guard's neck as the man fell. He lay back, his neck broken. Jessie had clambered over the wall as well, and now as the onslaught of peons continued, the *bandidos* fell back, racing for the shelter of the big house and its high walls.

There was sniper fire from the twin towers and from several of the upstairs windows, but by ducking behind its high walls and moving through the hedges and trees behind the house, very few casualties were suffered.

Ki was far in the lead as the army emerged from the trees to find the vast pit that had been dug in the yard: a vast pit with a forlorn legion of Indian slaves standing hopelessly near it and a contingent of well-armed guards.

The men of San Ignacio wasted no time for once. Bursting from the trees and following in Ki's footsteps, they opened up on the guards. Gunfire racked the guards' bodies. They tried futilely to fight back, but they were overmatched.

Ki saw an Indian slave break free of the group he was standing with, snatch up a dead guard's rifle, and fire it into the body. Jessica was kneeling, carefully picking her targets. Her ears were filled with the roar of the guns. Acrid smoke burned her nostrils.

Still, she was steady enough to pick off one fleeing guard, to see him stumble and topple into the pit dug for the slaves. She glanced toward the house, reloading automatically. There was little fire coming from the windows on this side. If they could breach the wall and reach the house, there was a good chance they could finish this.

She rose and trotted to where Ki stood, his face immobile and eyes set, as he stared at the dead, at the grim crater in the ground. Other slaves were arming themselves and gathering around Diego who instructed them.

"Ki," Jessie said, taking his arm, "if we strike now, we can win."

"Yes." Still, Ki had that far away look in his eyes, a grim reflection of the terrible slaughter around them. He blinked away his meditative mood and his eyes came alert again. "Diego, take your Indians and half of our people. Surround the house. Don't let anyone out. I won't take a chance on Brecht escaping now."

"No one will escape," Diego promised.

"Jessica, I want you to stay with Diego."

"Not a chance, Ki," the blonde said. Ki didn't try to argue with her. He had never had much luck in that department.

"All right. You men, we're going to climb that wall. Watch yourselves. There'll be *bandidos* in the windows once they know what we're up to. Six men. You men, watch the windows and keep their heads down."

He turned to Jess one last time, "Jessica—"

"Let's go, Ki," was her terse answer.

"Keep your head down," he growled. Ki was armed now. There was a place for firearms. This was it. He checked the loads in the Winchester repeater he had collected and nodded to his soldiers.

"One minute. Wait until the house is surrounded."

Diego had already led his men out, hurrying them back through the trees and around the far side of the house, stringing them out to form a deadly picket line. Ki gave him another two minutes.

"Now," he said nearly under his breath, and Ki started

loping toward the house, graceful and silent, weaving through the shadows as gunfire erupted again from somewhere in front of the house.

As Ki reached the wall, someone opened up from an upstairs window. A man beside him staggered and went down. Ki's sharpshooters laid down a hail of bullets at the window. They heard glass shatter and saw a *bandido* fall from the second story.

Ki turned, cupped his hands, and boosted up his first soldier. A second man followed, and then Ki leaped up, caught the edge of the wall, and rolled over, dropping to the courtyard beyond as the rifles from the house opened up again.

In a crouch Ki ran to the wall of the house and pressed himself against it. Jessica Starbuck was running toward him now, zigzagging to where Ki waited, his chest rising and falling steadily.

Two overeager peons were trying the back door, battering at it with their rifle butts.

"No!" Ki cried out a warning, but it was too late. Bullets from inside tore through the oaken door. One of the peons staggered backward, pawing at his face where a mass of heavy splinters had embedded themselves in his flesh. The other man never moved. His head had been blown away.

Ki looked to the wall where his men were now swarming into the courtyard; then he nodded at the window behind him. "I'm going in, Jessica."

Ki raised his rifle and fired through the curtained window four times. They heard a muffled moan and then a thud. Ki smashed the remaining glass from the frame and stepped over the sill, rolling into the room, his rifle ready. But the room was empty, except for the bullet-riddled bandit on the floor.

Jessica was into the room now, eyes flashing, rifle muzzle searching for a target.

Ki jabbed a finger in the direction of an inner door,

and they started that way, crossing a deep red, expensive Turkish rug that was now bloody and passing heavy dark oak cabinets and a gilt table set with candelabra.

Ki was on one side of the door, and as Jessica pressed herself against the wall on the other side, he kicked it open, drawing a spate of gunfire from the other side.

Crouching, Ki stepped into the doorway and returned the fire.One bandit stood at the foot of a long curving staircase, rifle on the floor before him, his hands futilely trying to hold his guts in. His eyes empty; his face etched with pain.

"Where is he?" Ki said to the man, shaking his arm and feeling only anger toward the badly wounded warrior. "Where is Brecht?"

"Brecht?" the *bandido* repeated and blood frothed from his lips.

"Don Alejandro," Jessica said, "where is Don Alejandro?"

"Up . . ." the *bandido*'s arm lifted, gestured vaguely up the stair case, and then fell as the man died, falling to the tile floor. Ki's eyes lifted to the stairs and he smiled faintly, ferally.

He glanced at Jessie, considered asking her to stay below, and discarded the idea. Her own eyes gleamed with the need to find Brecht, to find this cartel thug and finish him.

Ki started cautiously up the stairs keeping close to the wall and low. A door opened above, and from out of the darkness, a gun blasted three times, sending Ki to the floor. From behind him, Jessica's rifle spoke and the door was slammed shut again.

After glancing at Jessie, Ki started toward the landing. A single lamp illuminated the stairs softly. Outside, the guns continued to fire, their reports only small popping sounds inside the thick-walled house.

Ki stopped abruptly and lifted his head. He smelled smoke.

He turned and looked at Jessica who eyes had narrowed. She smelled it, too. Ki reached the landing on all fours and then rose sharply to his feet. Smoke was billowing from beneath the heavy door before him.

Ki moved to the door and kicked at it. A shot rang out, smacking dully into the wood. "Brecht!" he called out and again a gun fired. Ki kicked at the door again. The smoke was thick now in the hallway, and touching the door, Ki could feel the heat within.

He backed off quickly and just in time. The door caught like kindling, exploding into flame, and in seconds the landing was engulfed in twisting, angry red fire.

"Get back, Jessica; the house is on fire!"

"Brecht's in there," she shouted back.

"If he is, he's dead. We'll be dead as well if we don't clear out. Now!"

Ki felt the fire against his flesh, smelled his own hair singeing as he returned to the staircase, grabbed Jessie's arm, and started toward the outer door. The flames behind them moved like a whirlwind of fire, sweeping down the stairwell. In what seemed a matter of seconds, the entire upper story of the house was engulfed in flames. Smoke clotted the lower story as well. Ki still had Jessie's arm as he fought through the firestorm and smoke toward a window. He kicked it out and they rolled through, breathing fresh air in deeply.

Ki glanced up. It was no good. The entire house was going. He could smell the coal oil in the smoke clearly. Brecht had planned ahead. When he saw which way the battle was going, he had splashed fuel oil throughout the house and then struck a match. Now Brecht was going up in flames, wrapped in crackling fiery tongues of his own funeral pyre.

"God," Jessica said, "what a way to go!"

"Pity for the man?" Ki asked stiffly.

"For anyone who goes that way, Ki. Never mind—let's go."

As they crossed the courtyard, something upstairs gave, and with a shuddering moan, half the second story floor fell, caving in to send sparks and flames out the windows and leaping into the night sky like a vast, vengeful torch. Jessie and Ki climbed the wall again and returned to the pit. There Diego, Maria, and the remainder of the peon army stood in awe, watching the house burn, crumble, sag, and die.

★

Chapter 21

Around Jessica Starbuck and Ki, the cheers sounded as loud as the roaring of flames. The night was bright with fire, alive with high spirits. The people of San Ignacio broke into impromptu dances, and this time Maria had no reason to scold them for their joy. This time their was nothing to diminish their joy.

The Indians stood in small groups, some still clinging tensely to their captured weapons.

"What is it they want?" Ki asked Diego.

"Permission, perhaps? Permission to go, to leave this place of horrors."

"They don't need our permission to do anything," Ki answered. "Tell them to go wherever they choose, to do as they like."

"Diego," Jessica Starbuck said, "tell them one more thing. Tell the Papagos that they had a great warrior among them, a man much responsible for saving their lives. Tell them that they must honor the memory of Fly Catcher."

Diego nodded and walked off to talk to the Indians. Maria clung to Ki's arm, tearful yet smiling. Jessica stood alone for a long while, listening to the flames and watching the great house die as the flames went out. There was only the moon above the vast desert then, its cool light soft and peaceful.

"Let's go," she finally said to Ki. "I don't want to watch this anymore."

Ki was surprised. "No? I thought you would enjoy this moment, Jessica. It's over now, all over."

"Not over, Ki. You know it and I know it. Sometimes I wonder if it will ever be over."

Ki didn't answer. He left her to her thoughts. Jessica Starbuck turned, sighing. Then she walked slowly away from the scene of destruction. On a night like this, she thought, on an endless empty night like this one . . . but Marshal Longarm, her special someone, was far away. She could only walk on as the pale moon rose over the destroyed cartel house.

Watch for

LONE STAR AND THE GUNPOWDER CURE

forty-seventh novel in the exciting
LONE STAR
series from Jove

coming in July!